Worthy's Town

Worthy's Town

Sharon Rolens

Bridge Works Publishing Company
Bridgehampton, New York

Published in the United States by Bridge Works Publishing Company,
Bridgehampton, New York. Distributed in the United States by
National Book Network, Lanham, Maryland.

Special thanks to Alexandra Shelley and Barbara Phillips, two talented and
patient editors.

For descriptions of this and other Bridge Works books visit the Web site of
National Book Network at www.nbnbooks.com.

FIRST EDITION

The characters and events in this book are fictitious. Any similarity to actual
persons, living or dead, is coincidental and not intended by the author.

Library of Congress Cataloging-in-Publication Data

Rolens, Sharon.
    Worthy's town : a novel / Sharon Rolens. — 1st ed.
        p.   cm.
    ISBN 1-882593-35-9 (alk. paper)
    1. Illegitimate children — Fiction.   2. City and town life — Fiction.
3. Grandparents — Fiction.   4. Birthfathers — Fiction.   5. Illinois —
Fiction.   6. Authors — Fiction.   I. Title.

PS3568.O53328   W6   2000
813'.54 — dc21   00-033723

2   4   6   8   10   9   7   5   3   1

Jacket and book design by Eva Auchincloss
Jacket imaging by Jennifer Wallis

Printed in the United States of America

For Darwin, who encouraged me to write this book

Much as I own I owe
The passers of the past
Because their to and fro
Has cut this road to last

— *Robert Frost, from "Closed for Good"*

Prologue

In January, 1925, not one man among the five hundred citizens of Old Kane, Illinois, was without a job unless he wanted to be. Some found work at the local ball bat factory or grain elevator, and some worked at the cartridge factory in Alton or the oil refinery in Wood River. Others managed to engage themselves profitably in enterprises of their own ingenuity: raising night crawlers, breeding and selling raccoons for pets or pelts, playing musical instruments for round and square dances. Booze, stilled to perfection, continued to bring a good price; the favorite carrying place was the heel of a shoe, or a flask formfitted to a lady's thigh. Dairy farmers and feed growers, getting along tolerably since the prosperous war years ended, filled out the remainder of Greene County's countryside.

Outsiders looking at Old Kane might have thought life moved at a snail's pace, but to the people who lived there, events came one after the other with hardly a breath between. Given the choice of living any place in the country, each man, woman and child would have chosen to stay in Old Kane.

Of all the farmers around Old Kane, Worthy Giberson was one of the most respected — known throughout the county for his honesty and hard work. Not once did he sell a cow suspected of coming down with the mad staggers, nor did he ever trade a horse that was showing signs of being stringhalted. Worthy always gave a fair deal and expected the same in return. He raised his boy, Cappy, in that tradition.

Part I

Chapter I

At age forty-nine, Willa Giberson suddenly found herself with her daughter Chastity's newborn to raise. From an instinct all but forgotten, she put the squalling infant to one thin breast. Like any newborn animal, it knew to suck. Willa's breasts began to fill with a colorless fluid, an occurrence known as the "wet-nurse phenomenon," and by the end of the first week the fluid had turned chalky white. Just as she had thought she was slowing down, her monthlies coming only now and then, she found herself thrust back into mothering.

"It appears we're in the soup," Worthy said, as he watched his wife trying to quiet the crying baby. "I figured at our age we was through diapering babies."

"It must of been God's Will, it sure wasn't mine," Willa said, still surprised to find a red, wrinkled infant lying in her lap. "But he's here, and I'm already taken with him."

"I can tell that by just looking at the two of you together." Worthy's usual noncommittal expression began to take on some of its old youthful pride. He pondered a moment. "Who's to say? Maybe having a young one underfoot will keep us on our toes. Leastwise we won't have time to set and rock. I reckon you'll get first turn at the boy, he needs to start out with a mother, and somewhere down the road I'll take over. I'm game if you are."

Willa sighed. "I never was good at saying no."

The baby began to cry louder. Seems he's always hungry, Willa thought as she put him to her breast again. She leaned back in the rocking chair and closed her eyes, allowing random memories of Chastity to rush over her as they so often did these days. Was it only two short years ago that Chastity had come to her with those first awful fears? She easily recalled the incident — still so vivid in her mind.

WILLA HAD BEEN IN THE CELLAR, waist high in dirty clothes, when Chastity approached her. Tears ran down the girl's face as she stood in front of her mother, and between sobs began telling what had happened overnight.

"Ma, there's something bad wrong with me. My sheet — it's covered with bloody spots and I've got this funny hurting in my stomach. What do you think's the matter, Ma? Do I have to see Doc Potter?" She looked at Willa expectantly, fearing the worst.

Willa had believed there was plenty of time before her twelve-year-old daughter would come sick. Girls grow up faster nowadays, she thought sadly, searching for words to explain Chastity's malady.

"It's not so bad as it first seems," Willa said, as she tried to calm her anxious daughter. "It's just another of God's punishments for women — because of Eve and her sinful ways with Adam. It happens to every girl."

"But what does it mean?" Chastity sobbed.

"It means your body's ready to produce babies, but the rest of you is barely past playing with dolls."

"Will it come again, the bleeding?" Chastity asked, her sobs beginning to lessen.

"Once a moon," Willa had said as she piled a basket high with wet clothes ready for the line. "And there are some rules that go with it. Make sure not to take a bath during your time, and especially don't run or jump or wash your head." She handed the girl a gray rag from the rag bag. "Pin this to your underwear and be sure to rinch it out every night. Otherwise you'll be drawing boys."

"But Ma, there's something else. I get these strange feelings that come every night when I'm trying to go to sleep. Even counting sheep won't make them go away." She was on the verge of tears again.

Willa knew what was going on with her daughter. When she was a girl herself it had taken all her efforts to suppress those nightly urgings. "What you're feeling is normal for a girl of twelve," she said, "but you need to curtail such yearnings till your wedding night. Men don't like an easy quality in a wife." Willa had been surprised to hear her own mother's words coming out of her mouth.

WILLA WAS NOT A WOMAN GIVEN to looking deep into life. Raised a Hard Shell Baptist, she learned never to question when good or bad came about, God's Great Plan being of necessity hidden from mortals, women in particular. When she first learned her daughter, only fourteen years old, was with child, she accepted it as God's Work, though she could not understand His motive. More than once, when Chastity was carrying the baby but not yet showing, Willa had asked her to name the father, but the girl only shrugged her shoulders and went mute.

Willa had dreaded telling Worthy, but on hearing of their daughter's predicament he merely said, "Now don't that cap all!" — the only words passed between them on the subject. (When it was time to name the baby, those words returned to Willa. "Cap Giberson, he'll be called, Cappy for short." She repeated the name until it felt natural to her tongue.)

Neither Willa nor Worthy had known how desperately Chastity tried to discourage the unwanted thing growing inside her: spreading her legs and poking with Willa's number nine knitting needle; swallowing salts laced with a pinch of arsenic; pushing and prodding at her round little belly hoping to expel the squirmy growth. But Cappy would not be dissuaded. In spite of repeated affronts from sharp objects and bitter poisons, after eight long months inside Chastity's hostile body, he weighed eight pounds. On the morning of April 1, 1925, one well-placed kick sent Chastity's water spilling across the kitchen floor.

Willa called for Aunt Pearl, a self-taught midwife who lived in a lean-to near Coal Hollow. By the time the old woman arrived at the Giberson house with her bag of crude instruments and homemade potions, Chastity was screaming and thrashing in the bloody bed. Finally, after ten hours of birthing misery, one of Cappy's feet popped out. Aunt Pearl reached in with both grimy hands and pulled.

Chastity had taken one look at the wriggling baby and said to Willa, "You can have it."

Following the birth, Chastity lay in oblivion, her fever rising. On the third day Worthy sent for Doc Potter, but by then the child-bed fever had a firm hold. When her son was only three days old, Chastity died.

At the funeral, Brother Beams kept the mourners two hours. He expounded on God's Mercy and God's Love, and he even brought in the story of the Three Wise Men and the Prodigal Son. Chastity having been called home early was God's Will, he said, and therefore not to be argued with. She was no doubt looking down from Heaven at that very moment, wishing the entire family would soon join her.

Cappy, asleep in Willa's arms, loudly filled his diaper.

THAT NIGHT, as the mourning family was preparing for bed, a car drove up the lane and parked in front of the house. The driver impatiently honked the horn.

Worthy raised the window and yelled. "Who is it and what do you want at this ungodly hour?"

"Drayton R. Hunt. There's a matter that needs tending to."

"Can't it wait till daylight?"

"It sure as hell can't."

Generally, Worthy avoided Drayton Hunt, a bully by reputation and a bootlegger. As a boy, long before prohibi-tion, Drayton had been hired by his uncle to deliver bootleg liquor in townships that temperance advocates had already turned "dry", and after his uncle's death, he took over the lucrative business. By 1925, scotch was selling for $45 a case, beer for $30.

By the time Worthy was dressed and out the front door, Drayton was standing next to his elegant 1924 Moon; its idling engine emitted a low growl, its headlamps glowed like an alley cat's eyes. Drayton rested a hand on the open door, a lighted cigarette dangling from the corner of his mouth, his eyes defiant. Worthy noted Drayton's acne-scarred face, his tall, skinny frame.

"This better be good," Worthy said, as he approached Drayton. "I ain't in the best of moods after the day I've been through."

"Your recent grief is mainly why I'm here," Drayton said, snuffing out his cigarette and tossing it away. "It just may be I can ease your burden somewhat. You not being so young as you once was, or your good wife either, I've come to take that baby off your hands."

"Why in God's name would you offer such a thing? You ain't knowed for your kind works."

"Because that baby might just have some of my red blood running through his veins."

"What are you hinting at?" A chill went down Worthy's back.

"I ain't *hinting* at nothing, I'm stating a fact. I was well acquainted with that girl of yours, and now I've come to claim what's mine."

Worthy moved closer to Drayton and shouted directly in his face. "Get out of here, you son of a bitch, before I claim your hide! Am I getting through to you?"

Drayton spat close to Worthy's bare feet and wiped his mouth on his sleeve. "Sounds to me like you don't believe a word I said."

"You're damned right I don't, you bastard!"

"It appears I ain't the only bastard you're dealing with these days!"

Worthy's bowels turned to water as he pictured Drayton with his young daughter. Surely she wouldn't have willingly bedded with this piece of shit, he thought, but there's no way of knowing the truth.

"Believe what you want, it don't matter to me," Drayton said, "but that high and mighty daughter of yours was as hot for my pecker as a common whore. Dwell on *that* every time you look at her bastard baby!"

Worthy could have killed Drayton Hunt without a second thought, but he would not dishonor his daughter by dropping to Drayton's level. All he wanted was to end this talk and fall into bed. He took a step back. "You've said what you come to say, now get off my land."

"That suits me, but I'll be back." Drayton got into his motor car and roared out the lane, covering Worthy with his dust.

Worthy walked toward the well, sick with grief. After sitting through his daughter's funeral, he had thought the day couldn't get any worse. He dipped cold water from the bucket and drank slowly, feeling the cold go all the way down. He poured what was left in the dipper on top of his head.

Although Worthy did not want to believe Drayton's disturbing story, the implications were enough to ruin many nights of sleep. He would not add to Willa's sorrow by telling her the purpose of Hunt's visit. Worthy walked slowly back to the house, tired as if he had spent the day walking behind a plow.

IN THE DAYS AFTER THE FUNERAL, Worthy and Willa tried to make sense of their daughter's death. They each had regrets, even feelings of guilt, but neither blamed the other. After supper they sat together near the heating stove reminiscing about Chastity. Cappy, lying in his basket at Willa's feet, made small noises.

"What on earth did we do to earn such harsh judgment from God?" Willa asked, her face a constant frown these days. "I hardly ever raised my voice at her."

"Hell, Willa, we didn't watch her careful enough and some young buck coaxed her to lay with him. If that God of yours was paying attention, He would of stopped the act before it begun!"

"She sure was smart when it came to books," Willa said, not addressing Worthy's bitter remarks. "Remember how she wanted to be a schoolteacher?"

"I put the quietus to that notion. I blame that pinchy-faced old maid teacher for planting such lofty ideas in her head."

"She was always a Daddy's girl," Willa said, her memories of Chastity jumping from one incident to another. "Remember, Worthy, how you couldn't sit down without her climbing on your lap begging for a story?"

Worthy did remember. As a little girl Chastity had trailed after him while he fed the stock and did the milking. And on a hot summer evening when he went to the outhouse to sit, she would follow as far as the hollyhocks and wait patiently for him to finish so he could tell again her favorite story.

But he also remembered how overnight their relationship changed. When she had taken on the scent of a woman at only age twelve, he became embarrassed by any show of affection from her. He assumed a gruffness that neither father nor daughter understood, causing a growing distance between them.

The September that Chastity was to enter eighth grade, Worthy widened the gap further. He brought up the matter with Willa, certain she would agree with him as she did with all of his ideas.

"I've been thinking about the girl," he said. "She's already got as much schooling as you or me, and if she stays here to home, you could make good use of the help around the house and garden."

Willa remembered when her own mother had made the same decision, and how devastated she had been at being forced to leave school and her friends behind. She knew Chastity would feel the same. In that brief instant, Willa's hopes for her daughter went up in Worthy's smoke. "Are you thinking she should quit going?"

"That's what I'm thinking."

"She's awful smart, Worthy. She never brings home a grade under 95. Seems a pity somehow."

"I ain't arguing but what she's smart, but that don't change my thinking. You know as well as I do that females belong in the home, raising babies and cooking meals. The world would be in a sorry state of affairs if females forgot their place."

"I'll call her and see what she has to say about it," Willa said.

When Chastity heard her name being called, she reluctantly put aside her book and went downstairs. "Now what?" she asked through the screen door.

"Your ma and me has been thinking about your schooling," Worthy said, getting right to the matter, "and how you've had enough. More than likely you'll be a wife and ma someday, like your own ma, and it's time you stayed home and learned how to do womanly work."

"But Pa, I was counting on being a schoolteacher!" she cried. "Like Miss Self! She says I'm smart enough to go through high school, even college. I don't want to be a wife and ma!"

"You're too comely to wind up an old-maid schoolteacher —" But before he could finish his thought, she had stormed back up the stairs.

"I sure as hell wasn't expecting that!" Worthy said to Willa.

"I was, but you had to hear it for yourself." It won't seem right this September not buying her school shoes and books, Willa thought. Growing up a female wasn't easy.

WHEN CHASTITY DIDN'T ANSWER ROLL CALL the first day of school, Miss Self dropped in on the Gibersons. Thinking Chastity might be ill, she had brought along some books to occupy the girl's time. She slowed the car to make the sharp turn into the Giberson lane, carefully picking her way between the ducks and guinea hens, and coasted to a stop directly in front of the two-story, red tile farmhouse.

Worthy was sitting on the front stoop sharpening his knife, preparing to rid the late-summer lambs of their tails. He was not happy to see Miss Self. Not only had she disobeyed the laws of nature by not having a man to look after her, damned if she didn't drive a Model T Ford!

"Good afternoon, Mr. Giberson," she said. She tried to smile.

"Afternoon." Worthy did not look up from his work, his attention on drawing a fine edge to his blade.

"I noticed Chastity wasn't in school this morning. Is she sick?"

"No, she ain't sick."

"Then why was she absent?"

"Her ma and me figured she's had enough schooling. For a female," he added.

"But Mr. Giberson, she's my best pupil, especially in English. The stories she hands in show so much imagination and her grammar is flawless. I'm certain she would make a fine English teacher." She looked expectantly at Worthy.

"Meaning no disrespect, but women belong in the home, and if I have any say-so, that's where she'll stay."

"But a student like your daughter seldom comes along. She can answer a question before I finish asking —"

"I've spoke my piece." Worthy had run out of arguments, and was ready to end the conversation.

"Mr. Giberson, you aren't the first ignorant man I've had to confront, and you probably won't be the last," Miss Self said, her voice suddenly sharp. "Denying Chastity the opportunity to fulfill her God-given gift of intelligence is nothing short of criminal!"

EVEN NOW, TWO YEARS LATER, Worthy remembered the insult with anger. He had not been accustomed to hearing a woman raise her voice at him, and he had no intention that day of allowing Miss Self to get the better of him.

He stirred the dwindling fire and sat back in his easy chair, recalling the rest of the confrontation.

"Now you're getting to the crux of the matter," he had said to Miss Self, "placing the blame square where it belongs, direct on God's shoulders. That 'gift' as you call it should of been give to my thick-headed boy where it could of been put to good use. A man needs all the brains he can get if he aims to prosper in this world and take care of his womenfolk. Getting back to God, I ain't strong for the Bible, but I do know this much — God made females to be helpmates to men. Now if them females is off teaching school or the like, men come up suffering. And we both know that ain't what God had in mind." He stood. "My lambs is waiting."

"Here are some books I brought for Chastity," Miss Self said. "They're hers to keep." Her hands shook with anger as she put them on the porch steps.

"Self-righteous old maid," Worthy muttered, as he watched Miss Self crank the Model T and drive away.

Worthy did not waver from his decision. Chastity remained home where she learned to bake crusty bread and sew a fine hem and push the carpet sweeper and stretch lace curtains. But in the privacy of her room, she read the books Miss Self had brought until they fell apart.

Over the years, Worthy had not allowed himself to consider how her life might have turned out had he not interfered.

CAPPY STIRRED IN HIS BASKET. Willa picked him up and put him over her shoulder; she hummed softly.

"Time we was going to bed," Worthy said, standing up and stretching. "The fire's about out — I don't want Cappy getting the croup." He banked the fire for the night, and closed the damper.

"I'll be along shortly," Willa said. She rocked for another five minutes, and then slowly climbed the stairs to bed.

AT FIVE O'CLOCK THE NEXT MORNING, the alarm rang, but Willa burrowed deeper under the covers. Just a few minutes more, she thought, recalling the recent sad days, anticipating what lay ahead. Now the only female in a family of males, the care of the house and Cappy would be totally hers, at least while he was too young to help around the farm.

Feeling her forty-nine years, Willa crawled out of bed, tired from tending the colicky baby through the night. As babies will, at first light Cappy had fallen asleep. She bent over the crib railing and kissed his head; it smelled of baby powder and sleep.

Her black mourning dress was still lying across the back of the chair. Years before she had made the dress for the inevitable day she would become a widow, never dreaming she would wear it to her daughter's funeral. She shook out the wrinkles and hung it out of sight in the back of the closet.

Worthy and Tick, their eleven-year-old son, already up and halfway through chores, would be coming in soon expecting breakfast. But Willa was in no hurry to start cooking. She fluffed the duck-feather pillows and pulled up the faded "double wedding ring" quilt. For a moment she thought she heard Chastity's step in the hallway coming to help. But those sharing times were gone, she thought sadly — not part of God's scheme or He would not have taken her daughter from her after only fourteen short years. Of all the troubles Willa had experienced, losing Chastity was the most painful and the most puzzling. I may need some help getting through this tribulation, Willa said to God.

Keeping her back to the mirror, she took off her long flannel nightgown. She believed a woman's naked body was not meant to be looked at, even by her own eyes. In twenty-five years of marriage, Worthy had not once seen her naked.

Unlike most farm women, who bathed only on Saturday in preparation for the Saturday night picture show and Sunday morning worship, Willa performed her toilet daily. She poured cold water into a pan and quickly washed her body. After drying herself, she dusted talcum under her arms, and rubbed some between her legs for good measure. She put on a dress made from flowered feed sacks, and a clean apron of like material, black shoes that laced, and heavy cotton stockings. The stockings were too hot for spring wear, but they helped hide the bulging veins in her thick legs.

Willa stood back and studied her reflection in the mirror. A plump, plain woman with deep frown lines, and pale blue eyes that held no hint of humor, stared back at her. Even as a baby she hadn't been pretty, her mother had told her often enough. But pretty isn't everything, Willa thought in her own defense. (Had she told her own daughter that she was pretty? She couldn't remember.)

Willa smoothed her sparse gray hair into a tight bun and pinned in a matching net, giving her hair the look of dusty cobwebs. Once her hair had been like Chastity's, the color of golden corn shucks, and had been instrumental in drawing Worthy's first look. She recalled the play party where they had met and how they danced every reel, her long hair bouncing with each step. Worthy was still the best dancer in Greene County, though lately there had been neither time nor spirit for dancing.

Cappy was awake again and fussing. Willa changed his diaper and wrapped him in a light blanket against the early morning coolness. Balancing him on one shoulder, she carried him gingerly down the steep steps. "Twelve," she said out loud as she reached the bottom step. "Now what do you suppose caused *that* to come out of my mouth?"

Willa put Cappy in his basket and started breakfast. She stood at the cookstove frying fresh side meat and eggs, still puzzling over the number she had spoken for no apparent reason. She set the hot food on the table just as Worthy and Tick came in from the barn.

"One," Willa said, as they sat down to eat.

"One what?" Worthy asked. "Pass the side meat, Tick."

She thought for a minute. "One week since the funeral, I suppose."

AFTER BREAKFAST WAS OVER and the last dish washed and put away, Willa glanced at the kitchen curtains. The background was white, sprinkled with tiny pink flowers, but smoke from the cookstove had turned the white gray. These are due for the wash, she thought. "Fifty-six." Her hand flew to her mouth. "Land, what's happening to me?"

She looked again at the curtains and one by one counted the flowers. Fifty-six. Willa was worried; she was not inclined to talking to herself, as many lonely farm wives did. And how could she have known there were fifty-six flowers before she counted them? She sat at the kitchen table and read through the *Farmer's Almanac* to see if mention was made of the ailment. Two paragraphs were devoted to dropsy (acute and regular), and female complaints took several pages on both sides, but she found nothing that mentioned calling out numbers. I must be the only one with this problem, she thought, wondering why God had singled her out once again.

Finally she settled on a reason based on her Baptist background. God wants everything in His Kingdom to be counted, she thought, and He wants me to help with the counting. In exchange, He won't call me home before my time like He did Chastity. With Baptists all over the world talking to God, I'd best count out loud so He'll be sure to hear me.

Though not aware of it, Willa had been counting to herself for years. She could have recited the number of buds on the rose trellis the previous summer, or how many stitches were in her "double wedding ring" quilt, or the number of steps the mule took from home to town. The ritual had begun with her first pregnancy; counting the days until she would be delivered, counting the days until Worthy would again intrude himself into her body.

In her depression over losing Chastity, Willa's need to count became vocal. Now, not only did *she* know she was counting, so did Worthy and Tick.

"GOD, DOESN'T EXPECT STARS and blades of grass to be counted," she explained to Cappy, as she oiled him from head to toe with fresh-rendered lard. "And dove droppings, they can't be counted. Eye blinks can be counted. But not gnats." At nighttime, her day's work done, she would tiptoe through the house counting heads on pillows: Tick made one, Worthy two, Cappy's towhead made three, and her own head would make four when she could find time to lay it down. Sometimes she counted Chastity's empty pillow, saying "five" in a low voice to keep from waking Worthy.

AT HARVEST TIME THAT YEAR and with extra farmhands to cook for, Willa turned the care of the baby over to Tick. Every morning she pumped her breasts dry and filled two bottles with the warm, rich milk. She showed Tick how to prop the bottle so Cappy wouldn't suck air and get colic, and how to change his diaper without sticking the wriggling baby's bottom with a pin. Cappy soon learned that one loud cry would bring Tick running to his side.

Tick was happy with his new duties; they beat working in the fields hearing his pa yell orders at him like he was a goat. He didn't even mind changing the urine-smelling, soggy diapers. When he would accidentally touch Cappy's tiny penis, it would grow as straight and stiff as a tenpenny nail.

To feed the hungry farmhands coming in at noontime, Willa baked four pies — two fresh peach, two wild blackberry. She scrubbed seventy-two new red potatoes for boiling, fried five young roosters and opened two jars of last year's *Country Gentleman* sweet corn; four hundred and thirteen tiny white kernels were packed inside each blue jar.

One hundred eighty-three days since the funeral.

EVEN AFTER CAPPY OUTGREW DIAPERS, Tick, who had quit school after the fourth grade, continued caring for the boy. When Cappy began to walk, the two became inseparable, in spite of eleven years' difference. The first thing every morning, Cappy would set out looking for Tick, and once he found him, he would not leave his side until bedtime.

As soon as he could put words together, Cappy began asking questions. Worthy and Willa were too busy to attend to his growing curiosity, but Tick always had time. Though Worthy found his older son backward, Cappy believed that his big brother knew the answer to everything. In return, Tick reveled in the admiring attention from the boy, the only person in the house to give him credit. Teacher and pupil. A satisfying arrangement. Neither cared that Tick's answers usually missed the mark.

When Cappy was almost six, he and Tick were walking through the south pasture, and came upon the old ram mating with a ewe. Although Tick had witnessed such scenes many times, it was Cappy's first.

"Tick, look at that! What's Old Rammy doing?"

"He's fornicating."

"What's that?"

"It's when he pokes his peter inside her. That's what peters are for, to poke into something."

"I use mine for peeing out of," Cappy said.

"Someday you'll find something you want to poke it into."

"You're the smartest brother in the whole world," Cappy said, as they walked toward the woods, hand in hand.

Chapter II

As April 1, 1931 grew near, Cappy followed Willa around the house asking one question after another about what presents he might get, the kind of birthday cake she would bake, would he have to go to school now? — making it impossible for her to listen to her radio stories. She couldn't remember the last time she had heard *Easy Aces* all the way through.

When the big day finally arrived, Willa prepared Cappy's favorite food for his birthday supper — fried chicken, mashed potatoes, applesauce made from the last of the Macintosh apples — but he was too excited to eat.

"I ain't hungry," he said as he reluctantly joined the rest of the family at the supper table. "Can't I just have cake and presents?"

"No you can't," Willa said. "You have to eat your meat and potatoes first."

"But it's my birthday!"

"Don't act like a baby, Cap, you're six years old. Now eat your supper or there won't be any cake and presents." Against Cappy's objections, Willa filled his plate, but once he started to eat he forgot he wasn't hungry. He happily sucked four drumsticks clean, and put the bare bones at the side of his plate.

When the main course was finished, Willa carried in a tall devil's food cake with six candles atop the sticky white icing. Cappy took a big breath and blew out the flames.

"What did you wish for?" Tick asked. Now that he was helping Worthy with spring plowing, Tick had less time to spend with Cappy.

"I wished I was smart like you," Cappy said.

While Willa cut the cake, Cappy opened his presents: a box of pickup sticks, and a small pearl-handled pocketknife similar to the large knife Worthy carried. But Tick's present was Cappy's favorite: a smooth, brown buckeye to carry in his pocket and rub whenever he needed good luck.

In the years since Cappy's birth, Worthy had not directed more than a dozen words the boy's way. As his father before him, Worthy believed each animal, human or otherwise, was allotted a fixed number of breaths that had to last a lifetime, and it was best not to waste them on children. During the birthday meal, he had been quieter than usual, his eyes on the small blond boy. After the cake was eaten, Worthy stood up and banged the table for attention.

"Everybody pay close heed! Something of import has come to mind and I have a pronouncement to make. I've concluded the time has come for me to take over the raising of Cappy. He's overdue for having a man's hand." Willa, he continued, could keep on seeing the boy was clean and his clothes washed and ironed, but otherwise she was free to sew or cook or do whatever women were fond of doing without having Cappy underfoot.

Willa was caught unawares. She had not stopped grieving over Chastity, and she was secretly pleased to have Cappy around the house, helping fill the empty place. Thinking of Worthy's latest change, but not happy about it, she cleared the table and set a pan of dishwater on the stove to heat.

Tick was devastated. There were so many things he longed to teach Cappy, things the boy would never learn from Worthy. From now on he would be lucky to get a word in. "Shit, that caps that!" he muttered under his breath. He got up from the table and headed for the cow barn.

The next morning, chores and breakfast over, Worthy hitched Old Red, his ancient mule, to the wagon and drove away, with Cappy on the seat beside him. He did not notice a woebegone Tick standing alone in the yard. When Chastity died, Tick had assumed he would take her place in his parents' affections. But now Worthy had taken over Cappy, the last straw. "What's the use?" he said as he walked toward the barn.

"We'll be going the north way past the Biesemeyer place," Worthy explained to Cappy. "It's a little longer route, but well worth the extra time. I must of been by there a hundred times, but it's a sight I never tire of seeing."

Without prompting, the mule turned Prough's Corner and slowed, hoping to graze at the roadside as Worthy sometimes allowed. But with a chilly spring wind picking up from the north, Worthy chose not to dally.

"Can I get some candy bacon at the store?" Cappy asked.

"I ain't your ma, so don't be pestering me to buy this and buy that. Just keep your mind on the stories I'll be telling you and you'll learn something. I don't want to waste my breath for nothing."

"O. K., Pa."

"As I recall, it was five summers back when Turk Mowrey's Feed Store overbought yellow paint. Some slick salesman put one over on old Turk, that's for damned sure. He persuaded Turk as how yellow was overtaking red when it come to painting barns —"

"Can I hold the reins, Pa?"

"I reckon so, but if you don't flick Old Red around the ears now and then, he'll stop for a snooze. Well, Turk couldn't sell that yellow paint for love nor money and it was taking up space. He had since heard from that same slick salesman how the coming color for barns was green, and he aimed to lay in a supply of green paint. Turk ended up offering yellow paint free to whoever was willing to cart it off."

"I'm tired of holding the reins, Pa."

"I'll take 'em from here on in. You done a right fair job your first try. Now, you see, Radious Biesemeyer's always been one for a bargain, so he jumped at that free paint, yellow or not. In a week's time him and his four boys painted everything in sight a beautiful egg-yolk yellow. The house, barn, chicken coop, corn crib, his saw horses, ax handles, mailbox, even the outhouse. If it was standing still, they slapped a coat of yellow paint on it. We're coming up on it now. Just feast your eyes, boy," he said, pointing to the brilliant farm, "and see what a little imagining can do."

"Yellow," Cappy said happily.

The old wagon groaned and creaked over bumps and ruts; Cappy gripped the seat with both hands to keep from bouncing out.

"If your ma was along," Worthy said, "she'd be counting every pile of horse dung between here and home, poor woman. She ain't got you in on that foolishness, has she?"

"No, Pa, except for my toes. Ma says my shoes won't stay on if God was to take my toes away. So I count 'em every night after I pick out the dirt. There's five toes on each foot."

Starting into Old Kane proper, they passed Gano Walk's house. Gano's forty-year-old son, Burley, was standing by the fence, waving at whoever drove by. Burley was having a good day. Already he had waved at the ice wagon, the bread truck, and now Worthy, and it wasn't even ten o'clock.

"Wave your hand back," Worthy said. "Poor old Burley was shell-shocked while fighting across the waters. He ain't been right since."

"You mean a seashell like you hear the ocean in, Pa?"

"No, shell shock comes from a bombshell," Worthy explained. "The way Burley's pa tells the story, Burley was down in a foxhole taking a crap when them sons-a-bitching Huns set off a bombshell not ten feet away. It shocked the sense right out of him. And Gano says Burley ain't enjoyed a peaceful shit since." (Worthy wondered if his language was too coarse for a six-year-old, though it was likely Cappy had heard the words from Tick. Nevertheless, maybe he should hold back.)

The wagon bumped along the quiet streets and turned onto Main — a shady street three blocks long, lined on each side by family-owned businesses. They passed the post office where Lacey, the postmaster, stayed busy reading customers' postal cards; Oettle's Tavern with Buck, the owner, missing a leg lost to a fast Burlington freight; Mayor Dinghie Varble's house, painted only on the two sides that showed from the street.

On his own, the mule stopped in front of Pick's General Store. Worthy climbed down and tied the reins to a post; he lifted Cappy to the ground and headed for the store, the boy running hard against the cold April wind to keep up.

Pick had been supplying Old Kane with meat and staples for twenty years, as had his father before him; everyone who shopped at Pick's got a square deal. Because he resembled Santa Claus — round face and belly, eyeglasses low on his nose — it followed that Christmas Eve would find Pick dressed in a red flannel suit with white cotton whiskers glued to his clean-shaven face, handing out candy canes and oranges to children and adults alike at the Old Kane Baptist Church.

At one time or another each week, Pick came in contact with every household in and around Old Kane. Known for being closemouthed, he was privy to secrets even the Catholic priest in Jerseyville would not hear at confession. There was no Mrs. Pick Richards, although he had twice come close. At the last minute he determined the ladies were more interested in sharing his profits than his bed.

Unless it was planting or harvesting time, a group of farmers gathered every morning at Pick's for a free cup of coffee and a chance to catch up on the latest tittle. With that in mind, Pick kept chairs around the woodstove and a pot of coffee simmering, winter and summer. But on this particular morning, the store was empty. As it was unseasonably cold for April, Pick had built a roaring fire; the aroma of strong, fresh coffee filled the store building.

"Morning to you, Worthy," Pick said, getting out a heavy white cup, Worthy's favorite. "Sounds like March blowing out there instead of April."

"You got that right," Worthy said. He pulled off his gloves and warmed his hands over the hot stove. "There was times we wasn't touching the road for the wind whipping us."

Pick filled Worthy's cup, as well as one for himself. Worthy pulled a chair close to the fire and sat toasting his feet while he sipped the strong brew. "You know, Pick, outside of a good picture show, I'd as soon be setting here as anyplace I can think of. Speaking of picture shows, what's Dinghie playing this Saturday?" (Besides being mayor, Dinghie Varble owned and operated the Old Kane Picture Show.)

"Hard telling. Anymore you can't bank on what the sign out front says. Last week I went expecting to see *Monkey Business* but once I got inside it turned out to be *The Virginian*. He showed that old picture two years ago."

"Dinghie would post anything to get a crowd," Worthy said.

"I confronted him with the variance, and he said if he had posted *The Virginian* no one would of showed up. One thing for sure, this week before I pay my fifteen cents I intend to slip inside and make sure the picture matches the promise."

Cappy was standing with his nose pressed against the candy counter looking at the sweets.

"And who's this fine gentleman you've got with you?" Pick asked, turning his attention to Cappy. He had seen the boy hanging onto Willa's skirts, but this was the first time he had seen him with Worthy.

"He's a big butter-and-egg man from up North." Worthy looked proudly at Cappy. "He come by seeking work the other day, so I agreed to take him on. Claims he's stronger than he looks." Both men laughed.

"You know, I judge him to be a man who'd do a favor for a fella if that fella was to ask." Pick reached into the cooler. "It so happens I've got a special new kind of soda pop I need somebody reliable to try out. The salesman called it *lithiated lemon* but the bottle says *Seven Up*. How about it, boy?" Pick pried off the cap.

"O. K." Cappy reached for the frosty bottle.

"Say 'obliged' to Pick," Worthy said.

"Obliged." Cappy drank the cold soda slow to make it last.

"Just look at that yellow hair," Pick said, knuckling Cappy's head. "Sure favors Chastity, poor girl." He had always enjoyed it when she came to shop. She took her time looking at one thing and another, and she never once failed to ask after his health. Pick recalled one afternoon in particular when she had reached the store barely ahead of a sudden summer downpour. "Looks like you got here in the nick of time," he had said, smiling at the pretty girl.

She had smiled back. Cautiously she picked up a Ouija board, priced beyond her reach at eighty-seven cents, then quickly set it down.

"Well, now, what's your mama out of today?"

"Corn meal and lard."

"No doubt by now she's taught you all she knows about cooking and women's work. When the time comes, you'll make some young farmer a good and dutiful wife."

"Maybe I won't be a wife. I haven't made my mind up yet." She had looked longingly at the candy counter.

"Looks to be a good picture showing this Saturday night," Pick said. "*Beau Brummel* it's called."

"Ma likes to go for the free dishes. Two more shows and she'll have a whole set."

Pick had handed Chastity the sack of groceries.

It was around that time she stopped coming to his store altogether. Small wonder, Pick thought. "How's Willa doing these days?" he asked, turning his attention back to Worthy and Cappy.

"Still counting everything under the sun. It wouldn't be so damned aggravating if she counted to herself, but she says God might miss hearing her if she don't count out loud."

"The reason behind that counting has slipped my mind."

"It's pure foolishness, but she claims she was chose by God Himself to keep count of everything, and in return He wouldn't call her home before her time. It started back around the time — Cappy come along (he had almost said "when Chastity passed on" but caught himself), leastwise that's when I recall the folly first begun. Ain't it funny the turn a woman's mind can take?"

"They're not always easy to figure out, but then I'm no expert when it comes to the fair gender. How's that soda pop coming, mister?" he asked Cappy.

"It's coming good."

"I've took Cappy here under my wing for the rest of his upbringing," Worthy said, "but I'll tell you, Pick, my work's cut out for me. The boy's been in close surroundings with Willa and Tick for six years, well-meaning though they are. I hope his manliness ain't already stunted."

"Tick seems near to normal."

"If you don't look too close. When *he* was a tyke Willa let him grow like a jimsonweed, but with Cappy, she's forever pruning him back."

Pick added two seasoned hickory logs to the fire and refilled Worthy's cup. "Getting back to the subject of manliness, I can tell you how my pa made a man of me and it sure as hell took. He began by tossing me in the middle of Macoupin Creek one summer's day so I'd learn to swim."

"Willa would have a stroke if I threw Cappy in the creek; she's never held with her children learning to swim. But I've got an idea or two sifting through my brain."

"Good luck to you. Another fill-up?"

"Not today," Worthy said, noticing the darkening sky. "Give the man back his bottle, Cappy, so we can hightail it for home."

"Did you come in to make a buy?" Pick asked.

"It near slipped my mind. A package of Granger Rough Cut should do for today."

"Before you go, I've got something else new besides the soda pop." He held up a loaf of bread wrapped in shiny, cellophane paper. "Bread that comes already sliced and ready to hold a piece of meat. How about taking home a loaf and surprising Willa?"

CECIL COUNTY
PUBLIC LIBRARY
301 Newark Ave.
Elkton, MD 21921

"What'll they come up with next!" Worthy squeezed the bread for softness. "No thank you for taking any home. Women these days is spoiled enough. Give a woman spare time and she'll start coming into town to set and drink coffee like us men!"

"You might have something there," Pick agreed.

As Worthy and Cappy were turning to leave, Drayton Hunt entered. "Morning, fellas," he said pleasantly. He was dressed in a double-breasted suit, the gangster look popularized by James Cagney in *Public Enemy*. "Give me a pack of Luckies, Pick." He smiled at the small boy holding Worthy's hand. "Say, now, can this be who I think it is?"

"This is my boy, Cappy." Worthy had not come face to face with Drayton in three years. On Cappy's third birthday he had shown up on Worthy's doorstep trying to claim the boy once more. Worthy was dismayed now to see that Cappy and Drayton had the same dark brown eyes.

"He's fine looking." Drayton pinched the boy's cheek.

Seeing the gesture brought back Worthy's anger tenfold. If only I was twenty years younger, he thought. But he held his temper.

"Here, kid, I've got something for you." Drayton reached into his pocket and took out a dime.

Before Cappy could claim the coin, Worthy stopped him. "He don't need nothing from you, Hunt."

"Whatever you say, old man," Drayton replied. He dropped the dime back in his pocket. "Maybe some day I'll take him for a ride in my Moon. Would you like that, kid?"

"What's a Moon?"

"A Moon is a real special motorcar. Just ask your pa. He knows somebody who used to be real partial to my Moon."

"Watch your mouth," Worthy said, his fists clenched at his side.

"Whatever you say, old man," Drayton repeated. He paid for the cigarettes and left.

"What the hell was *that* all about?" Pick asked.

"Just something festering between him and me; I'll not go into it now." Worthy nodded toward Cappy.

"That one is bad news all the way around. I'd keep clear of him, if I was you. Mark my words, Drayton Hunt is headed for serious trouble."

"Thanks for the advice, but I'm well acquainted with him. Come on, Cap, we may beat the rains yet."

By the time the wagon reached the edge of town, low-lying clouds had opened up in a rainstorm mixed with sleet. Worthy and Cappy arrived home wet and cold all the way through. Worthy turned Cappy over to Willa and went upstairs to his bedroom.

Now I'll have the devil to pay, he thought, as he stripped off his wet clothes and rubbed himself with a towel. I'll likely as not come down with pneumonia over this excursion. Doc Potter will dose me with his homemade bitters and by the time the week's out, I'll be six feet deep. (Although Amos Potter had been trained at a respected medical school, his favorite cures came from bitter herbs and ginseng roots stirred together in his kitchen.)

Before Worthy put on dry overalls, he studied his reflection in the mirror, turning this way and that to get a full view. At fifty-seven he was holding his own, he determined; he still measured six feet, having not yet begun to shrink the way a woman does. His hair was coal black except for a touch of gray in his sideburns; already Willa's was as gray as his mother's when she passed on, he thought. But a woman don't hold her youth like a man, that's a given. Had it not been for his nose, wide and stubby, Worthy might have considered himself handsome.

Though not accustomed to thinking beyond the next crop of hogs, Worthy had begun considering his own mortality. There was a time not so long before when he could outrun, outwork, outfox any man in Greene County. His forefathers all lived well into their nineties, healthy until the day they died, but Worthy's body was slowing down. He was sure of it.

He believed his heart was wearing out; sometimes it would miss a beat and then race to catch up, just as it had done in his latest encounter with Drayton Hunt. And his eyes were growing steadily dimmer. He could barely pick off a quail or squirrel with his .22 rifle unless they were dozing. Every week when he scrubbed his head, hair was left standing in the washpan, no fewer than thirty black hairs each time. His manhood seldom grew hard anymore, and when it did stiffen some, by the time he rolled over on Willa, he was out of the notion.

Thinking of all his weaknesses, Worthy reasoned he was wasting valuable time hitching and unhitching his mule.

"What I need is a motorcar," he said after dinner. "One big enough to carry you and me and the boys to the picture show and back, or to church on Christmas and Easter. And we'd be out of the weather to boot," he added, recalling the drenching earlier. "Woman, go count up our money!"

Willa climbed the stairs to the bedroom; she stood on tiptoes to reach the top shelf of the closet where the money box was kept. (Since losing his entire savings of $155.14 when the Old Kane Bank failed, Worthy kept his money safe at home. And it gave Willa something to count.) She emptied the contents of the musty box onto the bed and counted out seventy-five dollars, all the cash they had after paying for the year's seed corn. She hoped that would be enough to buy a fairly good car.

Willa tried to imagine what it would be like having their own motorcar, the last family in the county to resist. Owning a car was undoubtedly costly; she would have to cut back on groceries for a while, but she was excited at the prospect of riding to town in comfort, no matter the season. Some of the town women drove by themselves, even on the hard road, but country women, other than Miss Self, left driving to the men and boys. Maybe she would talk to Worthy about teaching her, though she could guess his answer. She replaced the money box, empty except for a few buttons and snaps.

The next morning, Worthy and Tick hitched the unsuspecting mule to the wagon for its last trip to town and the entire family drove to Darr's Garage. Worthy handed Finice Darr seventy-five dollars and Finice handed Worthy the crank to a 1926 Chevrolet sedan, formerly owned by Radious Biesemeyer, hand-painted egg-yolk yellow.

"What about Old Red, Pa?" Cappy asked, as they all piled into the car.

"He'll find his way back to the barn."

"Snowflakes can't be counted," Willa said as they drove toward home, snow beginning to spit.

Chapter III

One sultry August evening that same year, Worthy was sitting on the front stoop enjoying his pipe and listening to the bullfrogs warm up for their nightly courting. Two whippoorwills a mile apart called back and forth, arranging a tryst.

Cappy sat at Worthy's side. A nervous lightning bug crawled up and down the boy's arm; he expertly removed the bug's light and added the glowing bit to his jar collection.

"Them birds make the loneliest sound in the world," Worthy said. "They can spoil a man's mood quicker than a bellyache." He blew a large smoke ring that floated in the heavy night air.

"Pa, who's Chastity?" Cappy asked, as he tossed away the remainder of the unfortunate insect.

Worthy nearly dropped his pipe. "What brought that up?"

"The man who give me the soda pop that day said I favor her."

"You've got a memory like a hawk. That was months back." Worthy squirmed like the hapless lightning bug.

"Who is she?" Cappy looked Worthy straight in the eye as he waited for the answer, a trick he'd learned from Worthy. ("If you want a truthful answer from a man, look him in the eye. If he looks up, down, or sidewise, you can bet he's about to tell a humdinger.")

For years, Worthy had been expecting that question, but he had hoped it would come later in Cappy's life. Now he was facing the question and the boy only six years of age. Damn you, Pick Richards!

"Well, Cap, if you're old enough to pose the question, you're old enough to hear the story. At least the bare bones of the story." He took a deep breath. "Here goes. The story starts before you come into being. You see, your ma and me, we used to have a daughter. She's who Pick was talking about. Chastity, we called her." This was the first time he had spoken his daughter's name in years.

"I had a sister?"

"Not exactly. The truth is — now don't let this throw you — she was your real ma."

"But . . . but . . . I thought *Ma* was my ma!"

"Willa *is* your ma if you mean who raised you, but your real ma was your ma's daughter. She died right after you was born. I always did blame that old midwife, Aunt Pearl, and her dirty hands. She got her start pulling the neighbors' calves and foals and went from there to babies." Worthy blew another smoke ring and watched as it floated away.

Cappy also sat quietly for a few minutes, trying to take in

Worthy's words. He poked a June bug with a stick, but decided not to mash it. "Are you my real pa?"

Worthy was slow with an answer. Cappy began to fidget.

"Well, in actual, I'm your grandpa."

"Who *is* my real pa?"

"I never heard so many questions at one setting. Your real pa ain't of no earthly consequence."

"You mean I didn't have one?"

"Of course you *had* one, you didn't sprout from no hollow log! I'm merely saying outside of doing the deed, your real pa wasn't of no earthly consequence!" Worthy raised his voice, something he seldom did with Cappy.

"How come you never told me you and Ma was not my real pa and ma?"

"Because you never broached the question. Now that you have, I'd be more than obliged if you forgot the issue. Your Ma is your ma and I'm your pa. Let it go at that."

"Was Chastity Tick's ma?"

"He was her brother!"

"Is Tick *my* brother, too?"

"Tick's your uncle. Damned if you wouldn't try a saint."

"Somebody's coming," Cappy said, jumping up as a noisy truck approached.

"Sounds like Bum Hetzel's old Ford. I wonder what's brewing in his pea brain." Saved by the bell, Worthy thought.

Since Bum's wife Imadean had died six years earlier, he was likely to turn up any place any time, not having any marital rules to follow. Friends since childhood, Bum and

Worthy still enjoyed each other's company, each man set on besting the other at storytelling.

"Evening to you," Worthy said, as Bum sauntered toward the porch, his limp hardly noticeable. One summer when he and Worthy were bucking bales, Bum fell off the wagon and broke his leg, leaving him with a shorter bum leg. The name "Bum" had stayed with him — as well as the limp.

Bum was no more than five feet tall, but he took advantage of every inch, keeping his back straight and his chin up like a bandmaster. A stranger might easily have mistaken him for a six-footer.

"Take a load off," Worthy said, happy to see his old friend.

"Believe I will." A smile spread across Bum's stubbled face when he noticed Cappy out of the house for a change; a boy's place was with his pa. "Who's your sidekick?"

"He's a new hand I've took on. Traded a sack of my best oats for him at the Carrollton Sale Barn last Saturday. It was either choose him or a banty rooster."

"You made a good choice." Bum pinched Cappy's ear, but not too hard. "And he won't be rousting you from a good sleep come sunup." He eased himself onto the step nearest Cappy and playfully offered the boy a chew of tobacco.

"I've got two little girls close to your size," Bum said to Cappy. "I won them in a crap game at Oettle's Tavern." Bum chuckled at his joke.

"What's on your mind this fine night?" Worthy asked. He drew deep on his pipe and filled the sticky evening air with more sweet smoke rings.

"I was out looking for wampus cats, but didn't have no luck. If it's in good condition, the tail off one is bringing upwards of six bits."

"What's a wampus cat, Pa?" Cappy asked.

"Worthy Giberson! Do you mean to set there and tell me this boy don't know about wampus cats?"

"That's the truth, he don't. I've been remiss," Worthy said, shaking his head in mock shame. "Come to think of it, he won't be allowed in first grade without no nice long tail to offer Miss Self come opening day."

"The longer the better!" Bum said. Both men laughed.

"What do you say to us figuring on a hunting trip tomorrow night?" Bum said. He looked directly at Cappy. "It'll be the light of the moon and wampus cats will be on the prowl looking for terrapins and toads to consume."

"My gut's been acting up lately," Worthy said, as he rubbed his belly, "but maybe I'll be up to going. What time was you thinking of?"

"Say nine o'clock?"

"Nine o'clock she is. But we won't be the only ones hunting wampus cats that hour of the night."

Bum lowered his voice to a whisper. "I wasn't wanting to scare the boy needless."

"Scare me of what?" Cappy's eyes widened.

"Woods witches will undoubted be out." Bum kept his voice low, but not so low that Cappy couldn't overhear. "They're famous for using wampus cat tails in their brew, the trouble being they sometimes throw in a tender juicy boy for extra taste. Just make sure you stick close to your pa or me once we get in the woods." He winked at Cappy. "Well, men, I'm heading home. Widow Prosser is tending my girls and I promised I'd not be away too long."

"The good widow ain't got her eye on you, has she?" Worthy asked.

"Which eye would you be referring to?"

Worthy laughed. "I forgot they don't jibe. Come to think of it, she might be the ideal woman for you, Bum. While her right eye was on washing dishes, her left eye could be watching your girls."

"If it's all the same to you, I plan to stay unbridled. I'll see you big hunters tomorrow night, and make sure the boy carries a gunnysack."

"What for?" Cappy was beginning to have serious doubts about the hunting trip.

"It's for slipping over your head once you spy a wampus cat," Bum explained, "so he won't see you and run off scared!"

"Can Tick go?" Cappy asked, believing there was safety in numbers.

"Tick's been before. It'll just be the three of us going."

As Bum drove away, Willa came out of the house carrying a five-gallon bucket of late green beans. "What was Bum after?" she asked, as she counted each bean snapped into her apron.

"He's thinking of joining up with a circus."

"Following the elephants with a shovel, no doubt."

BY NINE O'CLOCK THE NEXT NIGHT, Worthy and Cappy were ready and waiting for Bum. Worthy carried a lantern, Cappy clenched a gunnysack in his small hands.

"Ma says there ain't such things as woods witches and wampus cats," Cappy said. "She says you and Bum was storying." He wanted to believe her.

"That's like a woman, always trying to spoil us men's fun," Worthy laughed.

A pair of headlights turned into the lane and stopped in front of the house. Bum got out of his truck — a faded-green Ford with both bumpers wired on — and limped toward the house, his arms loaded with supplies. "I brought along some baloney to cook over the fire and some bread to put it on. Baloney is a wampus cat's favorite eating and the smell will help draw 'em out. You got your gunnysack, boy?"

"It's right here," Cappy said. He hugged the sack tight against his body, and felt in his pocket to make sure he had his lucky buckeye.

"Then let's head for the woods!"

"I thought you said we'd be hunting in the light of the moon," Worthy said. "The sky looks black as pitch to me."

"Never you worry, them clouds will pass. Before I left home, I inquired of the Ouija board."

The three hunters walked around the house to the back yard, passed through a field of corn stubble, and crossed the north pasture before coming to the stand of timber. As if on cue, the clouds disappeared and the full moon lit up the sky.

"What did I tell you!" Bum said. "I ain't knowed that board to mislead me yet! We'll head direct for a clearing by the branch and get a fire going so I can start the baloney to cooking. Before you can say 'jack-a-dandy' a pack of wampus cats will come running with them valuable tails stuck straight up at the moon!"

43

"I'll lead the way," Worthy said. Even with the full moon and his lantern, it was hard to pick a path through the dense woods. The two men fought their way through the tangled underbrush with Cappy struggling to keep up.

They walked twenty minutes before they reached the branch; even though it was August, it was running full, fed by a spring upstream. Bum gathered an armful of twigs and small sticks and he soon had a fire going. He pried a large oak log out of the ground to add to the fire, and exposed a patch of earth that glowed like red-hot embers. "Come here, boy! Quick!" Bum said, his voice excited. "This is something your average man don't often see!"

"What is it?" Cappy asked, looking down at the glow.

"Fox-fire!"

"You mean a fox made it?"

"Where it comes from, nobody knows for sure. You most generally find fox-fire hid beneath an old log or a rotting stump."

"Can you cook the baloney on it?"

"There's your other mystery, fox-fire ain't hot." Bum added the log to the flames; when the fire had burned down, he put several slices of baloney on a stick and held the meat over the coals. The aroma drifted through the trees.

Cappy was sitting on a stump no more than an inch from Worthy. "Where's the wampus cats? Ain't they coming?"

"Don't you worry," Bum said. "They're out there watching every move we make. They'll put in an appearance once their noses get a whiff of roasted baloney."

"Listen to them hootie owls hoot back and forth," Worthy whispered. "They're saying 'watch out for woods witches and wampus cats' in owl lingo." The owls hooted again.

"What'd they say this time, Pa?"

"They said, 'better keep that gunnysack handy'."

Even though the night was hot, Cappy shivered. "Can I try talking to them? In case I ever get lost?"

"Don't worry, Cap. If you was to get lost they'd let you in on what they was saying."

"Have some baloney, hot off the stick!" Bum said. He handed Worthy and Cappy each a piece of sizzling meat and thick-sliced bread.

"Don't mind if I do," Worthy said. He fixed a sandwich for himself and helped Cappy with his. Leaning back against a sassafras tree, he said, "Keep tonight in mind as you grow up, Cap. Life don't get no better than a man setting in the woods with his friend and his boy."

Cappy ate his sandwich, listening to the green firewood pop and crackle. He was still thinking about what Worthy had told him the night before about his real ma. He hadn't understood it all. Should he start calling Worthy "grandpa"? He wondered if Chastity had hunted wampus cats when she was little, or if only boys were allowed.

A slight breeze disturbed the tops of the tall trees; two tree frogs took up where the owls had left off; a small animal scurried through the leaves on the ground; nearby a fox screamed. Cappy moved in still closer to the two men.

"What does tonight remind you of, Bum?" Worthy shifted to find a comfortable spot on the log.

Bum thought for a minute. "Nothing comes direct to mind."

"That Halloween when we was boys played over again."

"Damned if it don't. I had put that clear out of my brain. It ain't something even a growed man wants to dwell on."

"What happened, Pa?" Cappy asked.

"Are you sure you want to hear the story? It ain't pretty."

Cappy's favorite pastime was listening to Worthy's stories, even scary ones. After only a brief hesitation, he said, "I want to hear it."

"There was a full moon same as tonight but no sooner would one cloud leave than another would follow in its stead. You couldn't depend from one breath till the next on seeing where you was going."

"Who all was there?" Cappy asked.

"Just me and Bum."

"If I'd suspicioned what was in store, I guarantee you I would of been somewheres else," Bum said.

"Well, me and Bum was planning on hunting weasels to earn some money for tobacco," Worthy went on. "Back then, weasel hides was in great demand by farmers, the hide being proof the weasel was no longer in need of their laying hens.

"After we had caught our first weasel, we found a spot in the woods to set and rest and relieve him of his hide. But before we could get around to it, the most god-awful racket started up — like half a dozen Brahma bulls tromping through the woods. We was too scared even to run off. The noise was getting closer and closer and all of a sudden was in our midst!"

Cappy grabbed Worthy's shirtsleeve. "What was it, Pa?"

"A wild man! He wasn't wearing no clothes and his hair reached clear to his behind. He looked to be a regular man, but there was one thing about him that was highly irregular. His foot, the left one if I rightly recall, was the longest foot on a human I had ever saw."

"That foot was the size of a canoe," Bum explained. "That's why he made so much commotion tromping through the woods."

"Was the wild man wanting to fight?" Cappy asked.

"After he got that growling out of his system, he told us he was aggravated because we was hunting weasels, them being mainly what he subsided on."

"What made his foot so long, Pa?" Cappy thought he could hear tromping in the woods behind him.

"The way he told it — he was about your age when it happened — he was picking blackberries so his ma could bake a pie and he stepped into a deep hole in the ground somewhere in the midst of a big woods. It was a year before a couple of coon hunters found him, and when they started pulling him out of the hole, his foot kept stretching and stretching till it was the size of a canoe, like Bum said."

"And when his folks took a look at that foot," Bum said, "they told him there wasn't room for him and his foot both in the house, so he would have to live out the rest of his days in the woods."

"Why was his folks so mean to him?"

"He didn't go into that, Cap. Anyway, we could tell his mouth was watering over that weasel carcass so we give it to him. The last we seen, he was tromping into the woods sucking on that weasel's hindmost leg."

"Well, the fire's about out and it's close to midnight," Bum said. "I'm for giving up on wampus cats this trip."

"But, Pa, you promised you'd get me a tail for school!" Cappy cried, tugging on Worthy's sleeve.

"We done our best, they just wasn't out tonight. Now let's head home, I'm wore out."

"Jesus Christ!" Cappy said.

"And what did I tell you about using them words? You'd better not let your ma hear such as that coming from your mouth."

"You say it all the time."

"That's different, I'm a growed man."

"You mean there's different words for growed men?"

"Hush up, or this is your last hunting trip."

"I'm ready, Pa." The argument forgotten, Cappy grabbed Worthy's hand on the chance Long Foot or wampus cats were watching.

"WELL, THE BOY FINALLY COME OUT with questions," Worthy said to Willa as they sat on the porch the next evening, Worthy with his pipe, Willa with her Bible.

"Surely you don't mean about mating and the like. I expected we had some years left before facing that grief. Here's something of interest — Chapter 119 of Psalms has 176 verses and the very next chapter has only seven."

"The questions wasn't about mating. They was about his real ma."

Willa stopped reading. "How'd the matter come up?"

"Back in April, that first day I took Cappy to town after his birthday, Pick had to go and say how Cappy has Chastity's looks. The boy's only now got around to posing questions."

"What did he say after you gave him the answers?"

"Every answer led to another question. Of course, I didn't give him *all* the answers. That wouldn't of been fitting."

"There's times I worry we've took on more than we can handle, Worthy, trying to raise a boy at our age, and it's likely the worst is yet to come."

Cappy came in from the chicken yard carrying a small frightened pullet. "Pa, how come chickens can't fly?" he asked as he spread its wings their full width.

"Chickens can fly. They just ain't interested in making the effort."

"If I had wings, I'd sure use 'em. I'd fly up to one of them fluffy clouds and roll around in it till I got tired. I expect that's where my real ma is, setting on a fluffy cloud. What did she look like, anyway?"

Willa took a minute to gather her thoughts. In the years since Chastity's death, she had willed herself not to speak the girl's name, hoping to forget the pain of losing her, the way a woman forgets the pain of childbirth. Even so, each day brought back a quick memory here and there: Cappy's thick blond hair, the color of Chastity's; the questioning nature they shared.

"Well, she was a right pretty girl," Willa began. "She had long yellow hair and a nice shape and the tiniest feet you ever saw. But sad to say that yellow hair and nice shape proved her downfall. If she'd been plain like other farm girls, maybe she wouldn't have got herself in the family way and died from it. She was willful from the start, had to have a store bottle." Willa laughed softly at the remembrance.

"Ma, can I see her picture and see for myself what she looked like?"

"I never got around to taking her picture, though I was always meaning to get a camera," Willa said, feeling the regret anew. "Time just got away from me. She'd be twenty years old by now. If you want to see what she looked like, just look in a mirror."

"Well, I'm ready to hit the hay." Worthy was always uncomfortable talking about the past. He stood up and scratched his arms and the back of his neck. "These damned mosquitoes is having a feast on me."

"I wonder how many times 'mosquito' is spoke in the Bible?" Willa said as she turned the thin pages.

"God was having a piss-poor day when he devised mosquitoes." Worthy knocked the ashes from his pipe and went inside.

"Time you was going to bed, too," Willa said to Cappy. Cappy sat sullenly. He was angry at her, and Worthy as well, although he didn't know why.

He returned the chicken to the coop, and then crawled into bed with all his clothes on, without saying his prayers — the most defiant act he could think of.

He dreamed about a girl with yellow hair but he couldn't make out her face. She was mad at him for causing her to be called home before her time. He awoke in the middle of the night crying, "I didn't mean to! I didn't mean to!" The temperature in the stuffy room was still in the nineties; he pulled off his sweaty clothes and stood in front of the open window, but the night breeze had already died down. He went back to bed and thought about his troubling dream. *Now I know what happens when you don't say your prayers.*

The bad dream aside, Cappy was not convinced of the worth of prayers. Night after night he had prayed for a bag of marbles like the beautiful ones in Bobby Garrett's tombstone at Jalappa Cemetery. Willa had explained that the little boy caught pneumonia and died, and his parents had his favorite marbles embedded in the tombstone in case he wanted to play with them. But once they were stuck in that stone, Bobby Garrett couldn't get them out if he wanted to. At least that's how it looked to Cappy.

But Cappy had other concerns. School was about to start, and no amount of praying would make it go away. He would be stuck sitting in White School for three or four years. Maybe if he could fool the teacher into thinking he was dumb, she would tell him he might as well stay home. It had worked for Tick. Cappy said a quick prayer (just in case) and slept soundly the rest of the night.

Chapter IV

By the time Cappy was ready to begin first grade at White School, he could tie both his shoes and gather eggs from the hen house — the extent of his early learning, Tick's tutoring notwithstanding. Some farm mothers taught their children to read before they started school, but Worthy had said, "That's why we pay the damned school teachers a thousand dollars a year!"

(Without Worthy's knowledge, Willa had taught Chastity to read from the *Farmer's Almanac* when she was only four.)

On the morning school was to begin, Worthy found Cappy sitting cross-legged in the middle of the kitchen table. "What's got into you, boy?"

"I ain't going."

"What do you mean, you ain't going?"

"I ain't going to school!"

"Well, you've got another think coming. Your ma has you decked out in brand new overhalls and high-tops, and I spent more than a dollar on your reading book. I say you're going!"

"But Pa, you said I had to take along a wampus cat's tail for the teacher, and I never got one. Tick says she's likely to be mad right off and whip me, so I ain't going!"

"Tick means well, but he don't always know what's what. As for the other, Bum and me conjured up that story about wampus cats and woods witches for fun. I didn't expect you'd take it to heart."

"You mean Ma was right? There ain't such things?"

"Your ma was right in a manner of speaking, but she's hampered by not having the Giberson imagination."

"What about Long Foot?" Cappy asked, fighting back tears.

"A story, plain and simple. Now, I want you to listen close to what I'm telling you. *Real* happenings in this life can be one pile of sheep turds after the other, and a story here and there makes them happenings easier to wade through. If you keep that in mind, everybody will like you and you'll wind up having some fun along the way."

"You all the time mix me up!" Cappy said, abruptly raising his voice. "First you tell me you're my pa, and then you ain't. And you tell me I need the tail off a wampus cat to take to school, and then you tell me there ain't such things as wampus cats! You tell me my ma was named Chastity! Someday I bet you'll tell me that was a story, too!" By then he was yelling.

"Calm down, boy, calm down. Let's go at this easy."

"How can I tell if something's a story or real?" Cappy was close to tears again, his face crimson. Worthy tried to pat the

53

boy's shoulder, but Cappy shrugged his hand away and stomped out the back door. How many times had Worthy seen Chastity do that very thing?

Worthy followed him, still trying to explain. "You can't tell if a story's real or not, and therein's the beauty. But we'll take this up another time when we ain't in a hurry. Now we'd best be going or you'll be late and the teacher may whip you after all."

On September 8, 1931, confused by recent revelations, Cappy reluctantly entered first grade at White School.

BY THE TIME CAPPY ARRIVED at the one-room schoolhouse, the singing of "America" and the pledging of allegiance were over. Miss Self led the wary boy to a small desk in the first row.

"This will be your desk until you outgrow it," she said, neither smiling nor frowning, her way with children and adults alike. "Tell your parents that you will need a tablet and pencil and also a box of eight wax crayons. If you have to go to the toilet, raise your right hand, one finger for number one, two fingers for — the other. This once, I'll put your dinner bucket away, but from now on you must take care of it yourself. If you get thirsty, there's a dipper and pail of water on a table beside the piano. Any questions?"

"Yes, ma'am. What if I have to do number one *and* the other?"

"Hold up your entire hand, I suppose." She had an uneasy feeling.

While Miss Self organized the day's lessons, Cappy looked around the room — his first time inside a schoolhouse. In one back corner, there was a large coal furnace (which the teacher was expected to keep going throughout the long winter), and in the opposite corner there were hooks for coats, and benches for boots and lunch buckets. Rows of small desks for the youngest pupils and double desks for the upper grades faced the teacher. Two large blackboards hung on one wall, and an old upright piano stood across the room.

Everything was new and bewildering, but what caught Cappy's eye most was a bookcase next to the piano that had books of every size and color. As far as he knew there were only two books in his house — a large black Bible that Willa read aloud from after Worthy had too much home brew, and the *Farmer's Almanac.* Cappy assumed the colorful books to be more tales about Jesus and God.

It didn't take long for Cappy to see that he was the smallest pupil in school, girls included. He could not imagine a worse predicament. Clearly he would have to figure something out or he would be lost in the crowd. And then he remembered Worthy's words about having fun along the way.

Before the lessons began, Miss Self asked each pupil to stand and say his or her name. When it was Cappy's turn, he stood as tall as he could and said, "Tick Giberson".

"But isn't that your brother's name?" she asked, remembering a dull Giberson boy who had quit school when he was ten.

"Yes, ma'am, but my pa liked the name so much he said I could have it, too." Everyone laughed — except Miss Self.

"According to my information, young man, your name is Cap Giberson, and Cap is the name I will use."

"Yes, ma'am."

"As this is the first day of school," she said, roll call finished, "I want each of you to write a paragraph about the most interesting thing you did over the summer. Those of you who cannot write may stand and tell what you did. I'll give you twenty minutes to complete the assignment, and then Hula May Simpkins may read hers first."

The pupils who could write began to do so, licking their pencil lead to make the writing dark. Cappy and the other first graders used the time deciding what they would say when it was their turn.

Hula May, a twelve-year-old girl taller than Miss Self, stood by the side of her desk. Over the summer her monthly flow had begun and her body was maturing rapidly. Most spectacular were her breasts, large and rounded with nipples so pointed they could easily poke holes in her shirtwaist.

"The most interesting thing I did last summer," Hula May began "was when my little sister Martha and I went to the St. Louis Zoo. Martha and I each ate three wieners and some cotton candy. After that Martha rode on the elephant but the man said I was too big so I stood and watched. All at once Martha threw up all over the elephant so they made her get off. Then we watched the monkeys pick bugs off each other. That is the most interesting thing I did last summer."

"It must have been a lovely trip," said Miss Self. "Cline Heberling, you may read next."

Cline was entering puberty less gracefully than Hula May. Pimples and blackheads covered his thin face and skinny back, and he had a particular odor about him that progressed as the day wore on. Most of the time he only pretended to wash, being embarrassed by his changing body, and when he did wash he didn't know to clean under his foreskin. Cline stood up, wanting desperately to dig at his crotch.

"The best thing I did this summer was go to my Uncle Bill's funeral in Haypress. The women cried a lot and the men told jokes and smoked Uncle Bill's best cigars. Uncle Bill looked fairly happy with a big grin on his face. My ma said the grin was the undertaker's work. Uncle Bill was too big for the coffin so the undertaker had to squeeze his shoulders together to make him fit. That was the most interesting thing I did this summer."

"Thank you, Cline." Miss Self covered her nose and mouth with a handkerchief. "Cline, how would you like to take the desk at the back of the room — next to the window?"

"Yes, ma'am, I would like that fine." He moved his belongings to his new desk, happy for the privacy to tend his bothersome itch.

"Cap Giberson."

Cappy stood and began to speak in a loud clear voice. "One morning I was throwing corn to the chickens and I heard a noise in the air and I looked up and seen this beautiful red airplane land in the back pasture. And the man flying it had a white scarf around his neck that blows in the wind, like at the picture show, and he had on glasses so bugs wouldn't get in his eyes. He said he looked down from the air and he thought maybe I would like a ride. I said I would, so the next thing we was up in the air. He said, 'How high do you want to take her?' and I said, 'High as she'll go.' So we went for the clouds. He said he was tired and would I fly for awhile. I was careful not to bump into a cloud and break a wing off. When it got dark we headed for the moon so we could see better and then we flew around the moon until almost time for the sun to come out. I said I didn't want to fly around the sun because it would be too hot. So we went back home and landed in the pasture."

"Young man! Where did you learn to tell such stories?"

"From my pa," Cappy said, proudly. "He says storytelling makes people happy."

"Well, it certainly doesn't make *me* happy. Now that you're in school, I won't have any storytelling or daydreaming, you're here to learn facts."

The rest of the pupils read or told their summer experiences, but Cappy judged his to be the best.

During first recess, in the midst of playing hide-and-seek, Cappy had to pee. He hurried toward the nearest tree, unbuttoning his overalls as he ran, and went in full view of the girls. They ran shrieking into the schoolhouse and told Miss Self, who marched outside to confront Cappy.

"Well, did you do it?" She scowled over the rims of her thick eyeglasses at the small blond boy.

"No, ma'am," he answered, buttoning up.

"Another story! Just for that, you'll stay in at recess every day for a month cleaning gum off desks and dusting erasers." Miss Self knew the circumstance of Cappy's birth and was disappointed to see he was so little like Chastity, the only pupil she had genuinely cared about in all her years of teaching.

Cappy had inherited chastity's intelligence, but in following Worthy's advice about storytelling (which he did to the letter), he never earned a mark above failing. If Miss Self asked him to write the sum of "2 + 2" on the blackboard, he would write "5" or "3" but not "4," which he knew to be the correct answer. If she asked him to stand and spell "cat," he would spell "d-o-g". Hearing the giggles around the room made the deception worthwhile.

At night while Worthy and Willa sat by the radio listening to *Death Valley Days*, Cappy was in his room practicing reading and arithmetic. Otherwise he might have inadvertently given a correct answer, and lost the respect of the other pupils.

At recess or noon, his storying became the primary source of entertainment.

"What's in your lunch bucket today?" Buzzy Jones would ask, grinning in anticipation.

"Boiled sheep brains and sour pickles."

Buzzy would bend over laughing and Cappy could feel himself growing taller.

"Where'd you get that new cap?" Hula May might ask, ready to laugh.

"The president of the United States sent it to me for my birthday."

"When's your birthday?"

"December 25, same as Jesus."

But Cappy's favorite story was of Chastity. He never tired of talking about her to anyone who would listen. "She was the most beautiful girl around Old Kane, with long yellow hair down her back —" he would begin.

"Where is she now?"

"She's in Hollywood in the moving pictures. She wanted to stay and take care of me, she loves me more than anything, but she said God expected her to be a moving picture star, that's why He made her beautiful and she couldn't be a moving picture star if she lived in Old Kane. At Christmas she sends me presents that cost lots of money. Some day I expect she'll come and take me to California."

Cappy would not remember when the story about his mother became truth to him.

AFTER A MONTH OF TOLERATING CAPPY'S HORSEPLAY in the schoolroom, Miss Self sent a note home asking Worthy and Willa to come to the school at four o'clock Friday to discuss the boy's deportment. They arrived on time, Willa in her Sunday best, Worthy in clean overalls. Miss Self briefly explained the problem.

"Damned if I see where's the problem," Worthy said, his skin prickling at being so close to Miss Self.

"The problem, Mr. Giberson, is Cap's absurd practice of making up a story when the truth would better serve."

"It does me good to hear he's chose that route so young in life," Worthy said, proudly. "My guess is he'll go far and have some good times along the way."

"Am I to understand you aren't perturbed with Cap's storytelling?" Miss Self asked.

"Where's the harm in dressing up the truth here and there? I've been known myself to add a bit to the facts now and then when the occasion called for it."

"But the boy tells lies!" she said, her face flushing pink. "That's not acceptable!"

"Oh, now, he ain't telling lies," Worthy insisted. "Cappy's brain takes the truth and turns it backwards front, which means it's the truth if you know how to read it. If he can come up with a way to ply that God-given gift, he'll be set for life!"

THREE WEEKS INTO SEPTEMBER, a new boy turned up for roll call. He was wearing bib overalls, the pant legs rolled up above his high-top shoes, and a red cap pulled down below his ears. He was even smaller than Cappy.

"Stand up and tell us your name and where you're from," said Miss Self, "but first take off your cap. Boys are never allowed to wear caps in school."

Reluctantly, the boy removed his cap to reveal a mass of wavy, black hair, a source of great embarrassment to the six-year-old. As he knew would happen, several girls giggled. Even with school beginning, his mother had refused to have his curls cut off. He had hoped wearing a cap would remove any doubt that he was a boy.

"My name is Beany Ozbun," he said, watching his feet, his voice low, "and we come here from Dow. I don't have no brother or sister, my ma says she's too poorly for any more of that business, and I live on a sheep farm with my folks."

"Very nice." Miss Self directed him to a desk behind Cappy. "I assume 'Beany' to be a nickname, and nicknames are forbidden in my schoolroom. I will need to know your given name."

"It's plain Bean," he said. "That was my ma's last name when she was a little girl."

But Miss Self seemed to have forgotten Beany. "Now, students, let's get busy and finish our work. A little bird told me this is the day the Coca-Cola truck might come. For the new pupils, the Coca-Cola truck visits all of the schools in Greene County once each year and gives everyone a free bottle of soda pop. Please remember to thank the driver, and please do not ask for more than one bottle."

During recess, Cappy took Beany in hand. He showed him the boys' toilet and explained the complicated rule of raising one or two fingers to alert Miss Self (and everyone else) as to the exact nature of his business. They joined a game of pitch and catch; Cappy was surprised to see that Beany could do neither, and when they played *olly olly oxin free,* he couldn't get the ball over the roof in a dozen tries. An only child, he had no one to play with; his father was busy in the fields or tending sheep, and his mother's delicate health did not allow her to leave the house except to see the doctor.

"What *can* you do?" Cappy asked, disappointed with his new friend.

"Nothing much." Beany was as disappointed as Cappy.

"It don't matter. You can come to my house every day after school, and I'll teach you them things." (If he could teach Beany to play well enough to join the games, Cappy would no longer be the last player chosen ahead of the girls.)

Just as the bell rang to end recess, a large truck turned into the drive and slowly climbed the steep hill to the schoolhouse. The driver stepped out and said in a loud voice,

"Is there anybody here at White School who wants a free, cold bottle of Coca-Cola?"

"I do," shouted all the children, and even Miss Self.

By the time the children had finished their sodas, gone to the toilet, and returned to their desks, it was past the time set aside for arithmetic. But no one complained.

EVERY DAY FOR THE REST OF THE SCHOOL YEAR and through the next summer, Cappy worked at teaching Beany to throw a baseball straight, hit it with a bat made from an oak stick, and throw the ball high enough to go over the schoolhouse roof on the first try. By the time school started in the fall, Beany had improved enough to join the games. Cappy was proud to see his protégé handle the ball almost as well as he did.

Toward the end of September, Cappy noticed that the other boys were avoiding Beany. He decided to ask Buzzy Jones, a knowledgeable third grader, why.

"He's a sissy, that's why," Buzzy explained.

"Why's he a sissy?" Cappy asked. "He plays pitch and catch or *run fox run* almost as good as me. I taught him myself," he said.

"He takes piano lessons, that's why."

"If that lie about him is true, how come he never told me? Me and him is best friends."

"Just ask him, I dare you."

Cappy and Beany were walking home together after school, throwing dirt clods at fence posts and taking turns tripping each other. They were unusually quiet.

Cappy spoke first. "Buzzy Jones says you take piano lessons."

"So?"

"Is it true, or was Buzzy telling a lie?"

"It's true. So what!"

"So how come I didn't know it and me being your best friend?"

"Shit! Do I have to tell you everything?"

"Shit! I don't care to know how many times you pee, but I'd ought to know something bad like you taking piano lessons!"

"So now you know I take piano lessons! So what!"

"I suppose it ain't your fault," Cappy said, giving his friend the benefit of the doubt. "Who's fault is it, anyway? Did you just start?"

"The idea of it was my ma's fault," Beany said, "and I started last Christmas."

"Why didn't you just say you wouldn't do it?"

"Maybe I didn't want to!"

"If my ma said for me to take piano lessons, I would just say I won't do it!"

"I'll tell you something but you can't tell Buzzy. You swear on the Bible?"

"I swear."

"Taking piano lessons is fun."

Cappy could not believe what he was hearing. "But piano lessons is for girls and sissies!" Cappy insisted.

"You read storybooks, even when you don't have to. If Buzzy and the others found out, they'd call you a sissy, too."

It was true, Cappy read everything he could get his hands on, sneaking storybooks from the schoolroom when Miss Self was looking out the window, and putting them back the next morning, read cover to cover. "Reading story-books is better than piano playing," Cappy said. He wished he could think of a reason.

"Piano playing is better than reading storybooks," Beany argued, not knowing why. "When the teacher ain't around, I play songs that ain't even my lesson, like 'Camptown Races' or 'Old Dan Tucker.' Sometimes I even make up my own songs!"

I'll sure keep *that* a secret, Cappy thought to himself. One thing about having a best friend, you have to like even the bad things about them.

Chapter V

Cappy and Beany became as inseparable as brothers. No matter what the season, they would hurry through chores to allow time together. Winter was the hardest, with snow and ice coming day or night without warning. And it was the depths of the depression, with farm products like wheat and corn finding fewer markets and every family member pitching in to survive the hard times. By the time the two boys did their chores, and trudged to school and back through snow drifts and over slick roads, there was little time for play.

But summer was a different matter. The days were longer. There was time to slip away to Macoupin Creek and lie on the bank, or put in a line hoping for a bluegill big enough to keep. Both boys were forbidden by their mothers to swim, a rule they abided by out of fear not only of their mothers, but also of God who (according to Brother Beams) was always watching out of the corner of His eye to see if they disobeyed their parents. Neither boy was willing to risk riling God for something as everyday as swimming even if, as Cappy suspected, He didn't exist.

One afternoon in 1933 they were lying on the bank, swatting the horse flies that crawled over them hungrily. "Let's get in the water," Cappy said. "I bet we can swim if we try."

"If our underwear's wet, our mas will know what we've been doing."

"We can take it off. Are you swimming or not?" Cappy pulled off his underwear and stuck his big toe into the warm water.

"I'm swimming." Beany followed Cappy's lead and waded in up to his waist.

Within a few minutes, they had enough nerve to go all the way into the water. They yelled and laughed as fish bumped playfully against their legs, the creek mud squishing between their toes. After a few tries, having swallowed several mouthsful of murky water, they were able to turn onto their backs and float. Tired and happy, they climbed onto the bank to lie in the sun and dry off. Both became good swimmers with their mothers none the wiser.

Toward the end of summer two years later the boys were at their usual spot on the creek bank, their clothes nearby.

Cappy was looking at the clouds. "Say, Beany, have you ever saw an eight-pager?"

"What is it?"

"It's a book that's got eight pages that shows cartoon people like Andy Gump or Dick Tracy doing stuff. Tick showed me his, he got it at the barbershop. One book shows

Dick Tracy doing stuff to his girlfriend, and her doing something weird to him. You ought to see it!"

"I'd like to, all right."

"Does your peter ever get hard yet? You know, like when you're trying to get to sleep?"

"Sometimes. Does yours?"

"Lots of times. It's hard right now."

"Let me see." Beany leaned close for a better look. "It looks hard all right."

"Want to feel of it?"

"Sure." He reached over and squeezed hard.

Both boys were quiet for a few minutes. Finally Beany said, "You can squeeze mine if you want to. It's not hard like yours, though."

"It's not so bad," Cappy said, gingerly touching his friend. "But I bet I can make it harder."

"How?"

"Something I seen in the eight-pager. Tick says it feels so good it hurts."

"So long as it don't hurt too bad."

Cappy leaned over and sucked Beany's small penis until it grew hard and straight. After a few minutes, he stopped to rest. "I told you I could make it hard. If you want to, you can suck mine. Just don't bite. Tick says it ruins the whole thing if you bite."

The rest of the afternoon they took turns; by the time they walked home, their mouths were as tired as if they had been sucking jawbreakers all day.

The next day at Macoupin Creek, Beany said, "Want to do what we done yesterday?"

"Nope," Cappy said.

"Me neither," said Beany. "Beat you into the water!"

IT WAS ONLY TUESDAY but Willa needed a few items from Pick's Store to tide her over until Saturday, her regular day for restocking the pantry. There was a time when Chastity had taken on that chore. Willa could still see her walking to town pulling Tick's play wagon behind her, a happy farm girl. Willa could not stop feeling at fault for the way her daughter's life turned out, though in all honesty, Chastity was partly to blame by giving in to temptation. But at least I've had Cappy for ten years, Willa thought.

Willa wrote out her list and handed it to Worthy who passed it to Cappy as soon as they left the house. Except for livestock feed or bags of manure, Worthy believed shopping was not a man's place. With that in mind, he took Cappy along to perform that female chore, allowing himself time for a quick stop at Oettle's Tavern. Cappy was handing the grocery list to Pick when the twenty-year-old Woosley Twins burst through the door.

Ralph and George Woosley were not real twins, with George having been born nine months after Ralph. The two boys were tall with identical round shoulders and hollow chests, and red curly hair all over their bodies — even on their toes. Ralph, the older, took the lead; when he quit school at the age of eleven, George soon followed. One twin was never seen without the other. It was rumored they sat together in the outhouse.

Cappy knew instinctively to keep out of the twins' way. While Pick was filling Willa's order, Cappy pretended to look through a display of shucking gloves on the counter. He meant to avoid eye contact with both men, much the way you would avoid eye contact with a vicious dog. The ploy worked with dogs, but not always with the Woosley Twins.

"Well, well," Ralph said, as he noticed Cappy, "if it ain't the little Giberson bastard. Let's see, his name is Carp? Cat? Clap! That's it. Clap Giberson. Named for his pa who carried around a case of the clap!"

"I hope you boys aren't here to cause trouble," Pick said. He tried to keep his voice pleasant.

"No trouble," George said, as polite as Pick. "We come to buy some *Maxwell House* for our ma. We're real fond of our ma, ain't that right, Ralph?"

"You bet we are," Ralph grinned. "Why, we're as fond of our ma as Clap Giberson is of his. Speaking of your ma, Clap, what's she doing these days? Still lolling around on them clouds? Or does she come to earth now and then to heat up some tramp's bed?"

"Tell your ma she can heat up my bed any time she pleases," George said. He made a loud sucking sound with his mouth.

"Here's your order," Pick said to Cappy. "Tell Willa she can pay the end of the week as usual."

"Say, George," Ralph said as he ruffled Cappy's hair, "I never noticed how pretty Clap here is. Ain't he pretty? He's every bit as pretty and blond as his Angel Ma was."

"Let's see if he's hiding a twat under them overhalls," George said. He grabbed for Cappy's crotch.

"You better leave me alone," Cappy said, backing away, "or my brother will beat you up!"

"Tick Giberson, now there's a twat for you!" said George, laughing loudly. "I bet he's setting in the barn right now trying to figure the way back to the house!"

"Here's your coffee, boys." Pick wanted to get their order out of the way so they would leave. "That'll be thirty cents."

"Just put it on Ma's ticket and she'll settle up the end of the month," George said. The twins left, laughing and making vulgar gestures with their fingers.

Pick made out a ticket for their purchase, bringing the Woosleys' bill to $54.06. He knew he would end up sending Sheriff Jesse Perdun to collect, and that the sheriff would come away empty-handed.

Cappy took the groceries to the car and waited for Worthy to satisfy his thirst. He couldn't stop thinking about the twins and the ugly things they had said, though he didn't understand it all. There had never been a time when Tick would have faced up to them, but it was all Cappy could think to say. "Sticks and stones can break my bones, but words can never harm me," went the children's rhyme. But Cappy knew the rhyme was wrong.

Late that night when Worthy was finished in the outhouse, Cappy was waiting by the hollyhocks, as Chastity had so often done. "She's all yours," Worthy said.

"I don't have to go, Pa, but I've got a question. I asked Tick about it but he said he stayed clear of that subject. It's about my real pa. Who is he, anyway? Does he live around here? Have I ever saw him?"

Worthy had expected Cappy to bring up the matter again. If only he had an answer that would satisfy the boy without giving the whole truth, or what he feared was the truth. "Did somebody say something?"

"Nobody said nothing, but everybody's got a pa but me. So I want to know who mine is."

"That's a hard question, Cap. Unless the guilty party comes forward and owns up, there's no sure way of finding out definite. And your real ma, she was too bashful to talk about such a private matter, even with Willa. Now here's another quandary. Even if some no-good confesses to being your pa, you can't go by that either, as men like to boast of fathering an offspring, especially an offspring like you turned out."

"To tell the truth, Pa, I don't so much care who he is, so long as he ain't a Woosley Twin."

"You can rest easy on that score, Cap."

"Thanks, Pa." Cappy went back to the house, satisfied for the time being.

Chapter VI

$\mathcal{A}$ week before eighth-grade commencement, Miss Self announced a contest for all upcoming graduates in Greene County sponsored by the *Democrat-Republican Patriot,* Carrollton's weekly newspaper. Pupils from the country grade schools — Swamp College, White School, Brushy, Mt. Gilead — and the town schools in Old Kane and Carrollton were asked to write an essay on "What I Learned in Eight Years of School" in twenty-five words or less, and send it in care of Asbury P. Wollums, Editor.

It would have been far more to the point to have written about the county's problems during the depression — dresses worn until they could no longer be repaired, ancient horses brought out of peaceful retirement to lead the plows. But Asbury Wollums's wife, Min, had thought up the idea. She believed in keeping the mood of the times light — her favorite song was "Life is Just a Bowl of Cherries" — and it was her money that had bought the *Patriot.*

First prize was a summer job at the newspaper, and the best essay would be published on the front page.

Miss Self handed entry forms to Mary Sue Dawdy, Jimmy Larson and Beany Ozbun, three of the four White School graduates, the fourth being Cappy. "I don't suppose you want one," she said to Cappy.

"Course not." But when she went outside to the toilet, he grabbed the entry form and slipped it into his dinner bucket, as she knew he would — a game they had played for eight years. Skeptical at first of Cappy's intelligence, she had come to understand him, and to grudgingly appreciate the mischief he used to hide his intelligence.

COMMENCEMENT EXERCISES AT WHITE SCHOOL came and went, with Jimmy and Mary Sue winning the citizenship awards. (Jimmy would puncture an eardrum with his mother's hat pin to avoid the draft four years later, and Mary Sue, a clerk at the Old Kane Post Office, would be caught carrying $2.57 in stamp money home in her pocketbook.)

Following the awards, diplomas were passed out that entitled each of the four pupils to advance to high school. Willa and Worthy sat in the front row, proud to see Cappy go so far in school — the first Giberson to do so.

But for Willa it was a bittersweet celebration. She had dreamed of seeing Chastity graduate, not only from eighth grade, but high school and maybe college. There had been no limit to her hopes for her daughter. Now those hopes were focused on Cappy.

ASBURY P. WOLLUMS fancied himself an author. Since finishing his English degree at Blackburn College ten years earlier, he had written four detective novels, all unpublished. When he learned that the Carrollton *Democrat-Republican Patriot* was on the selling block he put in a bid with his wife's money, seeing at last a way of getting his words in print. It had been eight years since the purchase contract was signed. Four hundred sixteen editorials later, Asbury P. Wollums was settled into small-town life.

ON A LATE WEDNESDAY NIGHT Asbury prepared to read the eighth-grade essays of the county children. The newspaper was due out each Friday morning, early enough for the rural mail carriers to deliver issues to farm families. Asbury had put off reading those damnable essays as long as possible, dreading the prattle of thirteen-year-old writing. He poured himself a cup of warmed-over coffee and prepared to read.

The first essay was by Harda Prill from Mt. Gilead School, written on lined yellow paper and decorated with drawings of violets: "I learned about arithmetic, orthography, spelling, and the history of what my forefathers did. On Fridays Mrs. Green taught we girls to paint our fingernails." If nothing else, she learned to count, Asbury thought. Twenty-five words on the nose. He laid the paper aside, starting a pile of rejects. He picked up the next essay.

"Because of the distinguished teaching of Mr. Theron Hanback, I have graduated with an excellent scholastic background. I shall continue my education through college. Respectfully, Frankie Linder, Old Kane School." Why, Franklin Linder, you old reprobate. Trying to pass off your writing as your nephew's. Onto the rejection pile.

"I did not lern shit. Yores truly, Shag Kallal, Brushy School." Poor kid, at least he's honest, Asbury thought — apparently they graduate everybody from Brushy School. The stack continued to grow.

Asbury read until midnight; the reject pile spilled off the desk. "There's got to be a better way to settle this," he said out loud, exhausted from the ordeal. He gathered all the essays, read and unread, and tossed them into the air; they scattered across the floor. He got down on his hands and knees, closed his eyes, and jabbed at the pile of papers with a letter opener. He picked up the skewered essay.

"In eight years I learned all the teacher threw at me. I even taught her a thing or two. Cap Giberson, White School."

"The winner!" Asbury laid the essay on top of his cluttered desk.

CAPPY WAS WAITING BY THE MAILBOX when the letter came. He started to open it, but instead he stuffed the letter down the front of his pants and ran to the house. Alone in his room, he sat on the edge of the bed staring at the envelope, afraid of what the letter inside would say. Finally, he tore open the envelope.

"Dear Cap Giberson:
Congratulations! Your essay, "What I Learned in Eight Years of
School", has won the contest.

Yours in Print,
Asbury P. Wollums,
Editor, Democrat-Republican Patriot."

Cappy whooped with joy. Besides the honor of winning the contest, he would have a summer job and earn his own spending money. He read the letter twice more, then hid it in a box beneath the bed with his other secret possessions: a postcard from Paris, France, picturing two plump girls, each with a hand on the other's buttocks; two nearly-new rubbers and a wiry, black hair Tick swore he had snatched from Maizie Plato's private place.

In his excitement, Cappy had forgotten that the hardest part was yet to come, convincing his parents to let him take the job. Worthy would be expecting him to help with the farming, as he had done every summer since he was ten. Willa would probably agree.

Eager to share his good news, Cappy walked to the Ozbun's house and knocked on the back door. Mrs. Ozbun peeked through the glass.

"Can I talk to Beany?" Cappy asked. He could hear the piano.

"Not until he's finished practicing," she said. "You can wait on the porch, but don't touch anything."

In all the years the boys had been friends, not once had Cappy been inside the Ozbun's house. It was a full thirty minutes before the piano stopped and Beany came outside.

"I won the essay contest!" Cappy said. "I'm on my way up in the world without having to go to high school!"

The question of high school had been a point of contention between the boys. Beany was going, so it followed that his best friend would go. But the Gibersons had never bothered with school after the eighth grade, Cappy insisted. He didn't know any reason to change that pattern.

"You damned dummy! Winning that contest is all the more reason to go!"

"And why are *you* going?" Cappy asked. "They sure as shit don't teach piano playing in high school."

"I want to know something to go along with piano playing!" Beany had raised his voice; he could not out-argue Cappy, but maybe he could out-yell him. "What did your folks say about the contest?" he asked, the flare-up over.

"I ain't told them yet. I'm saving the announcement to go along with supper. But Pa won't like me having a job. He never likes anything that's my idea. He'll say I need to stay and help farm."

"What about your ma?"

"If I point out how I'll be earning money, and how she can help me keep count of it, that might put her on my side. But she usually sides with Pa."

"I never knew you wanted to deliver newspapers," Beany said.

"It's not delivering newspapers, dummy, it's writing stories. I've been thinking about being a newspaper reporter ever since I watched *Front Page* at the picture show. I was keeping it a secret."

"Bean, dear, you've dawdled away nearly ten minutes," Mrs. Ozbun called. "Come in now and work on your études."

Cappy walked home through the alfalfa field, sorry for the life Beany lived.

THAT NIGHT AT THE SUPPER TABLE, Cappy finally got up his nerve. "Say, Pa, do you recall hearing about a contest being put on by the newspaper?"

"What newspaper would that be? Pass the peas, Tick."

"The *Democrat-Republican Patriot*. You know, the Carrollton paper."

"Never waste my time on it," Worthy said. He stirred his peas and mashed potatoes together, and covered the mixture with thick milk gravy.

"Just last week I read where Frieda Terpening and Dabs spent the day, Sunday I think it was, with Frieda's cousin over in Haypress," Willa said. "Five hours they were gone, if you count the time it took getting there and back. That was worth reading." She passed a dish of stewed rhubarb.

"It ain't called the *Weekly Wiper* for nothing," Worthy scoffed. "And that Asbury Wollums, coming from the big city the way he done, 'Ass-Bury' is what I call him. Thinks he's stirring with a big stick but he's barely rippling the surface."

"His wife's a little too plump," Willa said, not unkindly, "but she has a right pretty face. You never see her when she's not dressed up like it was Saturday night, high-heeled shoes and all."

"I got me a job at that paper!" Cappy blurted out.

"Sweeping up, I bet, that ain't nothing." Tick was painfully aware that Cappy had passed him by.

"What would they be having you do?" Willa asked.

"I'll be making up stories and writing them. That's what I'm best at. What do you think, Pa?"

Worthy rolled a biscuit around in his gravy and put it into his mouth whole; he waited until he had chewed and swallowed before answering. "I've been setting here giving the matter considerable contemplation, and as for sweeping up or carrying papers around to houses that wants one, you won't hear no objections from this corner. But when it comes to writing stories, I can't choke that down. I ain't having no boy of mine the butt of jokesters."

"But, Pa, you and Bum Hetzel tell stories all the time . . ."

"There's a hell of a difference in telling a story and putting one to paper."

"What's the difference?"

"I'll tell you what's the difference. The way I see it, your story *tellers* is worth their weight in gold, while your story *writers* add up to a dime a dozen. Outside of me and Bum, I can't call up the name of a solitary man in all of Greene County who can pass along a good story. We're a dying breed."

"Your grandpa on your pa's side was a storyteller," Willa said to Cappy, "and his pa before him. So your pa comes by it honest, and you too if the trait holds. It's worthy work — storytelling."

"But, Pa, a story is a story, whether you tell it or write it!"

"I've spoke my piece."

Cappy looked down at his plate, his appetite suddenly gone. Not that he was surprised at Worthy's reaction, it was more or less what he had expected. He thought the least Worthy could have said was "congratulations on winning the contest".

Conversation stopped. The only sounds were forks scraping across plates.

At last Willa said, "If you were to take that job, how would you be getting there?" She cut a sour-cream pie in fourths and passed the pieces around.

"I could walk to the hard road and take the bus. I'd be earning money, maybe even a dollar a week, so buying the ticket wouldn't be no problem."

"I say let the boy see what it's about," Willa said to Worthy. "A dollar can't be sneezed at."

"But I was counting on him and Tick to relieve me around the farm —"

"Maybe you'll have to hire a hand. That's not unheard of these days."

Worthy took his time eating his pie; he drank a glass of fresh, warm milk and wiped his mouth before speaking. "I guess it won't hurt to see what Ass-Bury has in mind. Could be it's delivering papers and I've got hot under the collar for naught." Although he would not let Cappy know how he felt, he was proud that the boy had ambitions, even if they weren't in the right direction.

Cappy could not believe that Worthy had relented, but he wouldn't question this unexpected stroke of luck. "Thanks,

Pa," Cappy grinned. "You won't be sorry." He dug into his supper with gusto.

The next morning cappy was up before the alarm. He went through the motions of eating the oatmeal Willa had cooked, but his stomach felt as if he had just stepped off a roundabout at the county fair. By seven-thirty he was standing at the highway waiting for the bus to Carrollton, uncomfortable in his Sunday clothes, his Sunday shoes pinching his feet from the two-mile walk.

Asbury P. Wollums also had arisen early, well ahead of sunup, well ahead of his wife. With a little forethought, he could manage an entire week without meeting Min face to face, but weekends were not so easy. He had an idea for another book, one about the editor of a small-town newspaper who was a detective in his spare time. That could easily keep him tied up Saturdays and Sundays for a year.

He sat at the kitchen table a few extra minutes with his coffee, relishing the quiet before the storm. Even with the paper coming out only once each week, most days he couldn't find time for a sandwich. Every day one of his employees had a gripe or wanted time off or complained because an article had not made the front page. Today, he faced dealing with his newly-divorced receptionist who had her eye on him, and his typesetter had set up a ten o'clock meeting, primed to ask for a raise in pay. Neither would get what they were after.

By the time he was settled behind his desk, someone was knocking on the door. "Come on in," he called.

Cappy pushed the door open. "Mr. Wollums?" he asked nervously, trying not to stare directly at the slight, balding man, "I'm the one that won the essay contest, you know, Cap Giberson?"

"What can I do for you?"

"I'm here about the job."

"Job?"

"You know, the job I'm to get for winning the contest."

Asbury had completely forgotten the promise of a job — maybe he could find something the kid could handle. "If you were to work here, when would you be ready to start?"

"I'm ready this very minute!"

"You're a little dressed up for work."

"I beg to differ, sir," Cappy said politely. "As you can see, I come dressed like a reporter dresses, like they do in the picture shows. Just tell me where to set and I'll get started reporting."

Asbury started to smile, but the boy was serious. "The job isn't being a reporter. Where in God's name did you get such an idea?"

"Seeing how I won a writing contest, I deduced the prize was a job writing. Ain't that right?"

"No, that 'ain't right'. How old are you anyway? Thirteen? Fourteen? What experience have you had? How much education? Can you even write a complete sentence?"

"I'm fourteen and I've had a lifetime of storytelling practice. I learned it firsthand from my pa, and I'm the best there is. Better than him, even. You can ask anybody around Old Kane. My teacher, Miss Self, in particular."

"There's more to newspaper reporting than being able to tell a story," Asbury said wearily, "it isn't something you wake up one morning and decide to do. Journalism takes years of study and experience, my boy. As for a job, the only one I have to offer is running errands to Day's Cafe for coffee and sandwiches, or the bus depot for cigarettes. There's no regular pay, you'd be working solely for tips. Through the summer you would work Monday through Saturday, but only Saturdays once school begins."

"I was intending to bypass high school and get straight to reporting —"

Asbury had heard enough. "If you want to work in the newspaper business you need four years of high school *and* four years of college. Come back and see me in eight years." Asbury stood up to signal the interview was over.

"When's my essay going to be in the paper?" Cappy asked. At least there was that to look forward to.

"Oh, yes, *The Essay*. If I were to publish it, we'd both be laughingstocks. You for writing it, me for printing it. Now, I need to get busy. Let me know if you want the job of runner."

"If my essay was so bad, how come it won the contest?" Could this day get any worse?

"Winning is sometimes a matter of luck, just let it go at that."

So much for the newspaper business, Cappy thought. From the way things were going, he would be stuck the rest of his life on the farm, shearing sheep and slopping hogs alongside Tick.

Cappy rode the next bus to Old Kane and walked the long way home past Radious Biesemeyer's fading egg-yolk yellow farm. By the time he reached the lane to his house, he had a large blister on each heel.

Cappy had not felt so bad since he was weaned.

ASBURY'S DISCOURAGING WORDS made Cappy more determined than ever to become a reporter. The *Democrat-
Republican Patriot* ain't the only newspaper in the state, he
thought. Jerseyville's got a weekly paper and Alton puts one
out every day. He began carrying a pencil and tablet, hoping
to overhear something he could write and submit. He would
show Asbury P. Wollums that he could write as well as a high
school or even a college graduate without wasting all those
years in school. And if Asbury wouldn't hire him, he'd try
one of the other newspapers.

With school out and the farm fields still too wet to
plant, Cappy first considered eavesdropping at the beauty
parlor, but chose Pick's Store instead where he could sit
behind the stove pretending to read a comic book. The
morning he chose to eavesdrop, four of Pick's regular coffee
drinkers — including Bum and Worthy — were gathered
around the stove waiting for the coffee to finish boiling.

"Jesus Christ, Pick," Worthy complained, "if you was to
start that goddamned coffee when you first got here, we
wouldn't have to set and twiddle our thumbs waiting!"

"I suppose you all heard what went on at the meeting hall
Thursday night?" Bum asked quickly, to change the subject.

"You mean Dinghie wanting to close down Kid Corner?"
Pick asked, filling cups around. "It'll never ride. Young people need a place to congregate on a Saturday night. Our good
mayor is getting narrow in his old age."

"That ain't what I'm talking about," Bum said. "It's them
Catholic Steinachers on the hard road. Them and others out
there has got a wild hare to start a 'new' Kane."

"What's wrong with *Old* Kane?" Worthy asked. "It's got everything a rational body could want — a bat factory, picture show, cafe with a duck pin alley, even a damned beauty saloon for the old hens."

"The Steinachers claim Old Kane is getting crowded," Bum said.

"Hell, that's easy to remedy," Worthy replied. "If the Steinachers stay out of Old Kane, there'll be nine less people crowding the sidewalks right off the bat."

"That wild hair about forming a new Kane probably goes back to the Pope," Bum said. "Him being across the waters, he don't know what's going on here."

"Them Steinachers is too damned good to come to church here in Old Kane," Worthy retorted. "Every Sunday, they drive all the way to Jerseyville."

"Do you think that's because the Catholic Church is located in Jerseyville?" Pick asked.

Cappy had heard enough. As he stood up to leave, Bum said, "I didn't see you hiding back there, Cap. What mischief are you up to?"

"Nothing, just writing down a few things."

"I thought school was out."

"Maybe he's writing sweet talk to some little girlie," said one of the other men, grinning at Cappy.

At that moment, Drayton Hunt swung open the front door, nearly knocking it off the hinges. Wearing a snappy single-breasted jacket of window-pane checks, he swaggered toward the group of men, grinning as he always did. He was still profiting from boot-legging. "Is this a private hog-cutting or can anybody join in?"

"It's not private, but we're out of seats," Pick said.

"You might think about adding a chair or two in the interest of your customers, Pick. Meanwhile, I'll just hoist myself up here." Settled on top of the counter, Drayton took a cigarette from his pocket and lit it. "Don't let me butt in, go on with what you was saying." Then he saw Cappy. "Well, I'll be goddamned, if it ain't Worthless Giberson's boy. He *is* your boy, ain't he, Worthless?" Drayton noticed that Cappy had shot up in growth, as tall as he had been at fourteen.

"Watch your tongue, Hunt!" Worthy bristled. He turned to Cappy and said, "Wait in the car. The air's starting to get foul in here —" Before he could finish the sentence, Cappy was out the door.

Drayton jumped down from the counter. "The last I heard it's still a free country, but I'm done here anyway. I've got better things to do than listen to you yokels." He abruptly left.

"I wouldn't put nothing past that bastard," Bum said.

"He's mostly mouth," Worthy said.

"How come you don't like drayton hunt?" Cappy asked Worthy on the road home.

"The son of a bitch is too mean to live. Enough said."

"He sure is ugly."

They rode the rest of the way in silence. After supper, Cappy sat in his room composing a short item.

POPE SAYS OLD KANE TOO CROWDED

The Herbert Steinacher family, the Catholics who live on the hard road, was told by the Pope to start a new town and call it "New Kane". Mayor Dinghie Varble thinks it is a good idea, and said that Kid Corner, which the Mayor thinks is getting to be a bother, can be moved from Old Kane to the New Kane. Mayor Varble looks to be against kids and in favor of Catholics.

The next day after school, Cappy rode the bus to Carrollton to show editor Wollums what he had written. He stood patiently by Asbury's desk waiting for a reaction, an expectant look on his face.

"What prompted you to write this?" Asbury was amused.

"It was news I heard with my own ears. You said that's what a good reporter does."

"I admire your tenacity, but I can't print hearsay." Asbury handed back the paper, suppressing a smile. "Without facts to back up a story, it's nothing more than gossip."

Cappy knew it was useless to argue. Asbury was the editor. Instead of eating lunch, he went to the library and looked up the word "tenacity". "Persistent; not easily pulled asunder". Cappy knew he had tenacity and then some.

Chapter VII

Offerings at the Old Kane Baptist Church began to steadily fall off in 1939, most people not yet recovered from the Great Depression. Brother Beams cut his salary in half, began eating only two meals a day, and replaced the forty-watt light bulbs in his study with fifteens. If something were not done soon to bring in fresh members and fresh money, he would be forced to reduce the amount pledged to missionaries in Africa. While he was willing to make necessary sacrifices himself, the work of saving the heathen souls had to go on.

Brother Beams was not the smartest preacher in the world, but he was one of the most conscientious. Every word he spoke from the pulpit was God's Truth as he knew it.

Nothing breathed life into a back-sliding church quicker than a week of spirited gospel meetings, and Brother Beams knew the best man for that job was The Reverend Art Gimmy of Exeter. Not only did the flashy evangelist have a flair for preaching the Word of God, he had a flair with the women, and it was the women who brought along the men — the only ones with cash. "Catch the cow and the bull comes along gentle." So, Brother Beams wasted no time in contacting the popular evangelist who agreed to lead the meeting. Once again the Reverend Art Gimmy, who had never seen the inside of a seminary, would spend a week rejuvenating the Old Kane Baptist Church and perhaps refurbishing his own pockets. To announce the revival, Brother Beams painted an even-dozen large red, white and blue signs.

Once the signs were posted, Willa counted the days. As Worthy had refused to teach her to drive, she would have to rely on him to see that she got to town every night. But as they were getting into the car to go to the first meeting, Worthy broke out with hives over his whole body. He returned to the house, happily scratching the large welts.

"I guess you'll be driving me," Willa said to Tick. "Find yourself a clean shirt and we'll be on our way. I need to get there in time for a back seat."

Tick, pleased that his mother was paying attention to him, went to his bedroom without a word of protest and put on his best, nearly-clean shirt.

"What about me?" Cappy asked.

"You can go," Willa said. "Three in a car brings good luck."

THE CHURCH DEACONS HAD SPENT THE DAY setting up a large tent in a cow pasture outside of town. By the time the three Gibersons arrived, the tent was nearly full. Folding chairs, borrowed from Linder's Undertaking Parlor, were lined up in rows, leaving a grassy aisle between. A portable organ had been set up close to the makeshift pulpit, and chairs for the two preachers completed the trappings on the small raised platform.

Willa, Tick and Cappy found seats in the back row next to the aisle. While they waited for the meeting to begin, Willa counted souls she deemed most in need of saving. (She did not count Jerry Loy who was saved anew at every revival.) "Fifteen!" she said out loud, causing several heads to turn her direction. Hoping to raise himself in his mother's eyes, Tick said "four", the number of holes in his teeth he could reach with the tip of his tongue.

On the chance that something interesting might happen, Cappy had brought along a pencil and tablet. He took a toothpick from his shirt pocket and put it in his mouth to chew on, the pencil he placed behind his left ear. Even if he wasn't yet a reporter, he could look the part.

The tent atmosphere reminded Cappy of a circus that had once come to town, but without the smells of roasted peanuts and cotton candy in the air. The air of excitement was the same — with the audience eagerly waiting for the stars of the show to make their appearance.

At seven-thirty, the organist began pumping a lively version of "That Old Time Religion". All heads turned toward the rear of the tent as the two men of God made their entrance. In spite of himself, Cappy found the excitement contagious; along with everyone else, he watched as the evangelist and Brother Beams paraded down the aisle.

The Reverend Art Gimmy was a marvel to see. He was tall, six feet or more, with an impressive shock of silvery hair. His mouth was sensual like a woman's, his teeth bright white. Before entering the tent, he had applied a touch of rouge to his smooth cheeks.

Brother Beams opened the meeting with a lengthy prayer; he was harshly critical of those who had allowed Satan to talk them out of worshipping in favor of Buck Oettle's Tavern or Dinghie Varble's picture show. The prayer elicited a number of "Amens".

"Six!" Willa whispered.

Following the prayer, the evangelist was introduced. He flashed a smile at the worshippers and said, "Friends, just call me Reverend Art! Now, let's everybody stand and sing praises to our Lord!" For fifteen minutes he led rousing revival choruses as foreplay to his sermon. When everyone was seated, heads bowed, he read several verses of scripture and offered a fervent prayer asking God Almighty to supply words to his tongue that would touch every wayward heart.

He began the sermon softly, but before he finished he could be heard five blocks away. While the organist softly played "Almost Persuaded", her eyes closed as she swayed on the organ stool, Reverend Art walked up and down the aisle. He waved his Bible in the air. He accused, pleaded, cajoled, threatened, seduced. The congregation began to squirm. Cappy took it all in, trying to think of a story line if he were to write about the revival. He scribbled some words on his tablet, then crossed them out. Maybe by the end of the week he would have something in mind. Until then, he would make notes of everything he heard and saw.

"Friends, tonight may be your final night on this wicked earth, you know that, don't you?" Reverend Art continued. "You may leave here and suffer a heart attack or get struck down by a stock truck. I don't want even one of you to walk away from here without Jesus sitting on your shoulder. So come on down front and take my hand. And I'm talking to you strong he-men out there, too. Nobody will make fun of you. Accepting Jesus as your Lord and Savior is like having a million-dollar insurance policy, friends. Reverend Art doesn't want a single soul to leave this tent before taking out their insurance policy on Heaven." He lowered his voice to a whisper. "Come on and give your heart to Jesus, right here, right now."

Cappy had heard the same words from Brother Beams, though not spoken with such passion. To please Willa, who feared for his soul, Cappy had tried to make sense of the promises and threats from the pulpit, but doubts lingered. He watched with interest as farmers and their wives walked down the aisle to repent.

Throughout the sermon, Cappy had been watching Tick out of the corner of his eye. His brother seemed hypnotized by the preacher's words. Usually he couldn't pay attention longer than ten minutes at a time. Cappy felt uneasy. Though he was much younger than Tick, he felt that his brother needed looking after.

When the invitation was nearly over, Tick felt the Hand of God on his left shoulder. It was in the form of a giant brown cockroach that had strolled into the tent. Reverend Art caught Tick's eye and saw signs of repentance, but Tick looked away. While Brother Beams dealt with the newly saved, Reverend Art stood at the back of the tent shaking hands. "Glad to have you in God's Tent, Sister," he said to Willa as he grasped both her hands.

"We'd be proud for you to come and eat, you and Brother Beams both, if you have a free night." Willa believed it was a Christian woman's duty to invite visiting clergy for supper.

"My dear lady, we'd be happy to sit at your blessed table. How about tomorrow night, say six o'clock?"

Cappy grimaced at the thought.

"That would do fine," Willa said. "Brother Beams knows where we live. Just tell him Worthy and Willa's place."

Willa spent the next day tidying the house and preparing supper. Worthy killed three young roosters to fry, and Willa baked an angel food cake topped with a pure white, seven-minute frosting. Devil's food was her favorite but that would not be proper to serve men of the cloth. By six o'clock, supper was on the table, all were seated, and Brother Beams had pronounced the blessing.

The guests ate greedily, barely taking a breath between bites and speaking only when they wanted more. They reminded Cappy of two hogs at a trough, filling their bellies as if there would never be another meal. Cappy's own food suddenly lost its taste.

"Well, Sister Giberson, that was a mighty fine meal, fit for the Lord Himself," Reverend Art said, wiping his mouth on Willa's best napkin and patting his firm belly.

"Yes," Brother Beams agreed. Away from the pulpit and the safety of platitudes, he found little to say.

"You have a fine family," Reverend Art said as he looked around the table. "Two fine-looking sons. But I don't recall your smiling face at the meeting," he said to Worthy. "I suppose you'll be going tonight?"

"You're supposing wrong. I don't hold with preaching, outside of a funeral now and then."

"I'm sorry you feel that way. But I'll pray for you, Brother Giberson, until you see the light." He turned to Tick. "And you, son, will you be in the House of the Lord tonight?"

Tick blushed, and looked at Willa for the answer. "Yes, he'll be driving me and Cappy," she said.

"It's a good son who sees after his mother. And I don't want to slight this young man," he said to Cappy. "God could use a good-looking lad like you carrying His banner."

"I'd a lot rather carry God's collection plate."

Willa gave Cappy a stern look.

"Well, friends," Reverend Art said, overlooking Cappy's impudence, "I'm loathe to leave this good company, but I like to get in a half-hour of praying before a meeting. God always has some last minute suggestions."

Cappy was relieved to see the men leaving. Between them they had eaten all of the drumsticks, and in two hours of talking neither man had said anything worth reporting for the paper. But it would be hard to prove anything a preacher said.

"By the way, Tick," Reverend Art said, "could I impose on you to carry my Bible to the car?"

"I don't mind." Tick felt a surge of pride at being singled out. The evangelist had been looking for a young man who could assist him in the pulpit, at the same time attracting the younger ladies. He saw in Tick the right combination of youth and gullibility, making him easy to mold in his own image. Perhaps with Tick's naiveté and country good looks,

The Ministry of the Reverend Art Gimmy could expand to include all of Illinois and part of Missouri. And maybe the boy could branch into healing. A good healer could swell a crowd — and the take.

Reverend Art lingered with Tick. "Son, I saw something in your eyes last night during the invitation. I saw a boy wanting Jesus. Was I right?"

"Maybe," Tick said. He stared at the ground, his hands in his pockets.

The evangelist put his hand on Tick's shoulder. "Son, tonight when I give the invitation, I want you to do something for me. I want you to say, 'Jesus, have your way with me. Jesus, I want to become a fisher of men. Jesus, I want to be like Reverend Art.' Will you think about it, son?"

"Yes."

He squeezed Tick's shoulder and climbed into the car beside Brother Beams.

Tick flushed; never had he been treated with such high regard except by Cappy. He stood watching as the car drove down the dusty lane and turned onto the gravel road. When he could no longer see the taillight, he went back inside to get ready for the meeting.

That night, as the organist played "Almost Persuaded", Tick Giberson walked down the center aisle and gave his life to Jesus.

Cappy and Willa waited outside the tent while Reverend Art talked to each convert, explaining the significance of their decision. Cappy could not think of a single sin that Tick needed forgiveness for. With his own doubts about the existence of God, Cappy hated to see his brother being taken for a ride when there was no driver at the wheel.

By the time Tick finally came out of the tent — his eyes red, his nose running — Cappy's anger had grown. "Now why did you go and do *that*?"

"I couldn't help myself," Tick said, blowing his nose. "Something got hold of me and drug me down front."

"That fool preacher is what got hold of you. Just wait till Pa finds out."

"He won't care one whit," Tick said. "Wait and see."

"I told you pa wouldn't care," Tick said to Cappy, "even when I said I was going with Reverend Art."

"But if you're not here, who will I ask when I need the answer to something? You know how closemouthed Pa is." Cappy no longer depended on Tick's answers, but he wouldn't let his brother know.

"You'll have to ask God, He's got the answers to every question in the world, seeing as He made the world and all the questions that go with it. If God don't answer, ask Jesus, he ain't so busy." Of his entire family, Tick would miss Cappy the most.

"Will you write letters telling me where you're at?" Cappy already knew the answer.

"You know I ain't much on writing, but I'll come back. Just save up all them questions."

On the final night of the revival, Tick packed his belongings in a brown paper sack and rode out of Old Kane with The Reverend Art Gimmy.

By MIDNIGHT, Reverend Art and Tick were well down the road to the next revival. They stopped at the first large town and stayed overnight in a cabin park; Reverend Art took the bed, Tick the roll-away.

"I don't feel right sleeping in this nice comfortable bed and you on that hard cot," Reverend Art said. "There's room in here for us both."

Tick climbed into the double bed and was nearly asleep when Reverend Art shook him by the shoulders.

"Son? My brain is so full of thinking about Jesus and all those sinners yet to save, I can't get to sleep. I need a massage, that's how my dear old mother would get me to sleep when I was a boy." Obediently, Tick rubbed the older man's back.

"You've got good hands for massaging, son. Now it's my turn. Roll over on your belly." He rubbed Tick's broad shoulders, then he eased the boy onto his back. He touched his lips to the boy's penis, lingering until it throbbed. He swallowed deep and wiped his mouth on the sheet.

"Thank you, son, for the nectar of our Loving God." Reverend Art snored loudly the rest of the night.

EARLY THE NEXT MORNING, the evangelist and his apprentice were on the road again; they stopped at a small diner for eggs and coffee. In the light of day, Reverend Art saw Tick's name as a hindrance. "What was your birth name, son?"

"William Worthy Giberson. Tick's my nickname."

"William could be shortened to Billy," The Reverend Art said, thinking out loud, "Billy is a good name for a man of the cloth." He regretted that his parents hadn't the foresight to name him Billy rather than Art, which had a secular ring. But he was superstitious about changing his own name so late in life. Then he remembered a name in a *Silver Screen* magazine that would go with "Billy".

"God has provided you with a new name," he said, pleased with the choice. "How does 'Billy Dupré' sound?"

"If it suits God, it suits me," answered the anointed Billy Dupré.

But Art Gimmy soon found he had a job on his hands shaping Billy Dupré into a preacher. Standing in front of a crowd, Billy couldn't put two words together without stammering. So he came up with the idea of having Billy speak in tongues, a sure crowd-pleaser.

Word of Billy Dupré and his ability to speak God's language soon spread over the state of Illinois. For the first time in its history, The Ministry of The Reverend Art Gimmy was booked twelve months in advance.

LATE ONE DAY IN JUNE, Cappy and Beany were fishing from the Macoupin Creek Bridge.

"Whatever happened to that job at the newspaper?" Beany asked.

"It was for running errands, not writing stories or news," Cappy said. "Winning that contest was a waste of time."

"If I tell you something, will you not jump all over me?" Beany asked.

"What is it?"

"I've got a job. It has to do with me and the piano."

"Are you playing at Oettle's?" Cappy knew that occasionally Oettle's Tavern had music on Saturday nights.

"No. I'm giving piano lessons." Beany held his breath waiting for Cappy's reaction.

"I can't believe it! Don't you know piano teachers are women? When this gets out, what are people going to think? Is this another one of your mother's ideas?"

"I get fifty cents for every lesson," Beany said. "Last week I gave ten lessons. What you or others think doesn't take away that five dollars in my pocket!"

"Five dollars? Are you joking?" Cappy frowned as he did the arithmetic in his head. "If you do that every week you'll be rich! I take back what I said, Beany. I wish I got that much for writing."

"You will, just keep practicing — wait, I've got a nibble!" Beany jerked the pole out of the water, a tiny bluegill swinging from the hook. The boys carefully removed the hook and tossed the fish back. The rest of the afternoon they sat without talking, sensing their carefree days were coming to a close.

Chapter VIII

If it hadn't been for Dimple Boston's breasts, Cappy would not have gone to high school. The first time Cappy saw Dimple, she was standing in line outside the Old Kane Picture Show. It was July and hot, but Dimple was wearing a red Angora sweater that clung to her like a wet bathing suit, partly because she was wet with perspiration underneath, and partly because she intentionally bought sweaters one size too small. By the time the double doors were unlocked to let in the crowd, Cappy was in the throes of love.

He bought his ticket and handed it to the ticket taker; the theater was nearly full, everyone scrambling for a place to sit. Cigarette smoke drifted lazily to the ceiling, and the smell of fresh-popped corn drenched with butter filled the air. Cappy gave the popcorn lady a nickel, and she handed him a large sack of popcorn. His mouth full of the salty treat, he stood at the door scanning the crowd until he found the girl in the red sweater. There were no seats next to her, so he settled for one across the aisle. Beany joined him. "How come you're sitting here in the back?"

"I've got my reasons," Cappy said.

Before the lights went out and the newsreel started, Cappy had time to stare at Dimple's magnificent breasts, high and pointed, stretching her sweater to its limit. Cappy could not keep his mind on the show, even though it starred Gary Cooper. Afterward he and Beany went to Mundy's for a hamburger sandwich, but all Cappy could think of was the girl in the red sweater.

The next day he asked around town and learned she was visiting her aunt who lived on Maple Street. By four o'clock that afternoon, Cappy was standing on the elderly lady's porch, knocking on the screen door.

Dimple answered. She was wearing white shorts and a snug pink sweater; her long brown hair was in neat braids, tied with pink ribbons. She stood waiting for him to speak.

Cappy was surprised at his nervousness. "My name's Cap Giberson, Cappy for short," he said.

"Mine's Dimple," she said, saving her smile.

"Since you're new in town, I thought to make your stay more enjoyable by letting you set with me in the picture show Saturday night."

"What's the picture?"

"Charlie Chan but I don't recall the title. There's likely to be a good deal of shooting."

"I don't like shows with shooting."

"You can't always go by the sign. For all I know, it might even be Deanna Durbin. The show starts at seven. I'll get there ahead and save you a seat."

"You mean I have to buy my own ticket?"

"Well —" This was a turn Cappy had not anticipated.

"City boys always buy a girl's ticket, if they expect you to sit with them — or anything."

"O. K. I'll meet you out front at 6:45 and we'll go in at the same time."

"What about popcorn?"

Even though Dinghie Varble, in an effort to help Old Kane citizens forget their troubles by lowering the price of movie admission, at ten cents for each ticket, plus a nickel for the popcorn, it appeared Cappy would be spending twenty-five cents on the evening. Dimple was worth the expense. "O. K., I'll buy popcorn. One sack. Myself, I don't much care for popcorn."

Dimple stood watching Cappy watch her. "You can't touch them, you know."

"Touch what?" His face turned as pink as Dimple's sweater.

"My attributes. That's what my mama calls them. You can look but not touch, not even if you pay for my ticket."

"Does this mean you'll go?"

"I guess so." She smiled, releasing two deep dimples.

By THE END OF JULY, Cappy had spent a dollar and fifty cents for the privilege of sitting next to Dimple on Saturday and Wednesday nights. Sometimes she let him feel her cotton panties, and once she let him touch the soft hair under the elastic. But her attributes remained taboo.

One Saturday night Dimple was sick. Cappy and Beany sat together in the front row as they had always done before

Dimple arrived. Beany kept his resentful feelings about Dimple to himself. It wouldn't do any good anyway, he lamented.

"Have you signed up for school yet?" Beany asked, as they waited for the newsreel to begin. He was determined not to let up on Cappy until he agreed to go to high school.

"I've had eight years of school, that's enough for anybody — especially a Giberson." Every time we're together Beany starts in, Cappy thought.

"Jimmy and Mary Sue are both going," Beany said. "That means you'll be the only one left behind. If I was you, I couldn't sleep knowing Jimmy Lawson was getting smarter every day and I was stuck with an eighth-grade brain."

Cappy didn't respond.

"How far have you got?" Beany asked, moving the subject to Dimple.

"Far enough."

"You afraid you won't know how to do it?" Both boys were virgins.

"Pa says when the time comes, I'll know what to do like I've been doing it all my life."

The lights dimmed and the boys leaned back in their seats to watch *Test Pilot*.

"Too bad Tick's not here," Cappy whispered. "He's crazy about airplane pictures. Now that he's a preacher, movies are probably a sin."

CAPPY'S PREOCCUPATION WITH DIMPLE seemed a natural thing to Worthy but Willa was concerned. He was near the age of Chastity's disaster. "Worthy, you need to talk to the boy."

"Hell, Willa, I did that years back."

"Maybe he ought to hear it again."

"There's no need, Cap's got a good head. In a week he'll have forgot all about that little tart."

But Cappy's interest in Dimple did not wane. By the end of summer, he had spent nearly four dollars on picture shows and popcorn. She was now meeting him in Jalappa Cemetery on a regular basis, agreeing to kissing and touching if he promised not to mess her hairdo — a pompadour she painstakingly pinned in place before every date. On one such occasion, he coaxed her out of her tight sweater and discovered her attributes were pieces of quilting cotton wadded into her brassiere. That deception endeared Dimple to Cappy even more.

One night as they sat waiting for the show to start, she said, "Mama says she and my daddy are getting a divorce, so I'll be staying with Aunt Maude until it's over. Then I'll go live with Mama."

Her words were cheerful enough, but her eyes were a little watery, Cappy thought. "I don't know anybody that's gotten a divorce," he said.

"Mama said they just got tired of being married."

"I'm sorry." He put his arm around Dimple's shoulders, even though the lights had not yet dimmed.

"You needn't be sorry. The good part is that I can go to high school right here in Old Kane. We'll be in the same class and we can see each other every single day. Won't that be fun?"

Cappy was the last to register for freshman class.

Chapter IX

⁓

Bank Night at the Old Kane Picture Show had proved a successful drawing card, with people crowding out front an hour before the doors opened, no matter what the picture, to make sure of a chance at the winnings.

The last Bank Night before school was to begin, Cappy and Dimple were in their usual seats waiting for the drawing. They each imagined how they would spend the money if they won the big twenty-five dollar prize: Dimple would spend her prize money on a cashmere sweater, and Cappy would buy a secondhand typewriter and teach himself how to type.

The first showing of *Love Finds Andy Hardy* had finished and the house lights were turned up. Dinghie entered from the back of the theater carrying the round tin can that held the names of prospective winners. He walked slowly down the aisle, the can held high above his head, as solemn as a priest preparing to offer the Holy Sacraments. When he reached the front, he turned to face the crowd and began to speak in a grand voice, like a stage actor, pausing between words for dramatic effect:

"As you all know — tonight — is Bank Night at — the Old Kane Picture Show. Three names — will be drawed — out. The prizes are five dollars — fifteen dollars — and twenty-five dollars —"

"For Christ's sake, Dinghie, get on with it!" someone yelled from the back. "We've heard that goddamned spiel a hundred times over!"

"We'll draw out the first name first, the second name second, and the third name third," Dinghie continued, unfazed by the interruption. "What little lady would like to assist me in drawing out the names?" Several small girls waved their hands, but Dinghie chose his chubby grand-daughter.

"The first name drawed out is Hank Simpson. Is Hank Simpson present?"

"You know good and well Hank Simpson's been dead and buried eight to ten years," Bum yelled from down front.

"So he has." Dinghie put Hank Simpson's name back into the can. "All right, we'll draw out the second name — Minnie Seely. Is Minnie Seely present?"

"Minnie moved to Haypress last year to live with her old-maid daughter," a lady in the third row said. "Say, Dinghie, why don't you take out the names of them that's moved away or died?"

"Getting on with the drawing, we'll now draw out the third name. And the third name drawed is Fred Weller. Is Fred Weller present?"

"Dammit, Dinghie, Fred's dead as a mutton steak!" everyone cried in unison.

"If Fred Weller's not amongst those present, it looks like there's no winner this week." Each week, everyone forgot that the only winner in the history of Bank Night had been Dinghie's wife, Salema, who spent her five-dollar windfall on a new Easter hat.

For ten years, the Woosley Twins had gone faithfully to Bank Night with nothing to show for their efforts. After another Wednesday night with no winners, they came up with a scheme. The two men jumped Dinghie, who was carrying the Bank Night drawing can to his car, tied a rag over his eyes, and taped his mouth shut. They pushed him inside the trunk and drove out of town.

At the time his mouth was taped shut, Dinghie had a wad of tobacco chewed just right for spitting. All he could do was swallow. (Salema later remarked that nothing's so bad that some good doesn't come from it, crediting the kidnappers with her husband's giving up tobacco-chewing.)

The twins drove to their father's farm and led the prisoner into a corner of the toolshed. First, they dumped the slips of paper onto the workbench. Between the two of them, they counted two hundred forty-eight names. "That does it, Ralph," George said, sweating heavily from the stress of counting.

"Now, George, we'll take two hundred forty-eight fresh pieces of paper and get to writing."

Both men wrote steadily for two hours. They carefully folded each paper and placed it inside the drawing can; when the can was full, they carried it to the car and set it on the back seat. They stuffed Dinghie inside the trunk, and returned to the alleyway, leaving the trunk ajar so he could escape on his own.

But Pick's regulars didn't believe Dinghie's story.

When Worthy came home telling of the kidnapping, Cappy listened carefully, sensing that he might benefit from Dinghie's misfortune. After supper he spent the evening writing. This time Asbury would surely take notice. He handed Asbury the sheet of handwritten words. "It's short, but it's a good story."

"But we don't publish stories, only news. How many times do I have to tell you?"

"You'll want to publish this one. It's a story and news both. It's about Dinghie Varble's kidnapping Wednesday night, right after the Bank Night drawing."

"I hadn't heard about that," Asbury said.

LOCAL MAN KIDNAPPED

Dinghie Varble is resting at his house after being kidnapped Wednesday night following the Bank Night drawing at which there was no winners. He was kidnapped by bullies who shoved him into the trunk of his own car, a Model A Ford, and taken out in the country. When he would not tell where his money was they dumped him in Macoupin Creek. He was fished out by Mr. Bum Hetzel who was trying to fish for bluegill. Cap Giberson, Star Reporter.

"And you're saying this is true?"

"I plumped it up here and there in the interest of better reading. Pa says your news items are dry as old bones."

"You can tell your father I value his opinion as much as that of a cow pie! Did you talk to Mayor Varble in person?"

"No, I got the information straight from Pa."

"Had *he* talked to the mayor?"

"No, Pa was in Pick's Store the morning after it happened, and that's where he heard the story."

"Rule number one in the newspaper business. You can't print a news item unless it's factual. The very least you could have done was interview Mayor Varble in person. If people want fiction, they read novels. Is any of this getting through to you?"

"It's getting through to me that I won't be getting any pay. Since I'm going to high school like you said I should, I figured you'd print my story in the way of showing good faith."

"High school's a good start, but only a start. Let me offer some advice. You can't write if you don't read. I'll give you some back issues of the paper. Go home and study them word for word until you get the feel of what newspaper writing is about."

"Since I won't be earning any money reporting, is that job of runner still open?"

"It's open. If you want it, be here by eight o'clock Saturday morning." Asbury handed Cappy a stack of old newspapers. Cappy stayed awake most of the night studying every word, even the want ads and death notices.

His first Saturday running errands, Cappy earned ninety-seven cents in tips. That night, besides a sack of popcorn for Dimple, he bought one for himself.

THE NEXT WEDNESDAY NIGHT, Dinghie Varble walked down the aisle carrying the Bank Night drawing can as if nothing untoward had taken place. "As you all know," he began, "tonight is Bank Night at the Old Kane Picture Show. I will dispense spelling the rules as you've all heard them before. The first name drawed will be for the five-dollar prize." His granddaughter reached into the can and drew out a slip of paper.

"The first name drawed is Ralph Woosley. Is Ralph Woosley present?"

"I sure as hell am!" Ralph called out. He strutted down the aisle like a bantam rooster. Dinghie handed Ralph a five-dollar bill and replaced his name in the can. "Thank you all for coming to the Old Kane Picture Show," Dinghie said. "Now Spider will run the second show for those who want to see it again."

At the next Bank Night, Dinghie skipped the preliminaries and went directly to reading the winning name. "This can't be right," he muttered to himself. "The winner of the five-dollar prize is Ralph Woosley," he said, his voice shaky. "Is Ralph Woosley present?"

"I'm setting right here!" Ralph strolled down the aisle and flourished a low bow. "Thank you kindly, Mr. Dinghie."

The following week, Dinghie reached into the can himself. The paper said, "Ralph Woosley."

"I reckon there's no doubt but what Ralph Woosley is present," Dinghie said, his tone lackluster. He reached into his pocket and took out five ones.

"Much obliged," Ralph said.

Drayton Hunt, in the audience that night as well as the two previous Wednesdays, watched the events with amusement. It appeared the Woosley Twins had a potential he hadn't recognized. He would remedy that oversight at the first opportunity.

After toting up tickets sold against prize money dispersed, no matter how Dinghie weighed it, Bank Night had become a losing proposition. He took the drawing can to the alleyway and dumped two hundred forty-eight pieces of paper onto the ground. A sudden breeze scattered Ralph Woosley's name all over Old Kane.

Part II

Chapter X

By spring of 1940, news of the trouble in Europe had worked its way to Greene County. Although rumblings of war had been on the radio and in the newspaper for months, no one expected events on the other side of the world to affect them one way or the other. In Old Kane, the first four months of the new year had not changed perceptibly from the previous year.

But life on the Giberson farm had changed drastically. With Tick somewhere in the Missouri hills courting sinners, and Cappy in high school and running errands at the newspaper, Worthy found it necessary to hire some help. Until now, no man who wasn't a Giberson, or at least a close friend, had put his hand to Giberson soil. But these were unusual times.

When he offered Shag Kallal, the best of the boys who applied, thirty-five cents an hour, the boy said, "My daddy says hold out for forty cents."

"How about this? Say you stick with the job for a month, I'll boost you to forty cents."

"I'm your man!"

Worthy stood watching the boy amble down the lane kicking a dung beetle ahead of him. "Times is getting hard, real hard," he said out loud, as he rubbed his aching shoulder. "A man spends his life raising boys, but there's never one around when you need him."

THERE HAD BEEN NO WORD FROM TICK since he left a year earlier. "Don't fret about Tick," Worthy said to Willa and Cappy with confidence he didn't feel. "When he gets that preaching out of his gullet, he'll come home dragging his tail behind him." So far Worthy had been wrong.

Besides worrying about her son, Willa was facing another problem; she was running out of things to count. There were only three people left under her own roof, and she had lost interest in tallying trees or birds on barbed-wire fences or feathers plucked from Sunday's roasting hen. Twice, she had tried giving up counting, but failed; counting was as much a part of her life as breathing. There was also her underlying fear of God's wrath if she quit counting without a good reason. But God provided by way of the United States government and the 1940 Census. The first census-taker hired in West Central Illinois was Willa Giberson.

Before beginning her new job, she carefully studied the census forms. There were questions about humans, but animals had been overlooked.

And there was the problem of Tick. Should he be counted, or not? Though his body was no longer in Greene County, most of his clothes still hung in the upstairs closet. Willa had worn a hole in the census form writing his name, erasing it, and writing it again. She solved the problem by writing a question mark.

By the end of the summer every person, as well as a good number of cats and dogs and one Poland China shoat, had been accounted for.

Willa's days had not been so fulfilled since she had been left with Cappy to raise.

CAPPY QUICKLY ADJUSTED TO HIGH SCHOOL, where he studied English, Algebra, World History and General Science. Study hall periods allowed ample time for students to prepare their next day's assignments, leaving the hours after school free. Cappy used all his free time to study big-city newspapers from St. Louis to Chicago, paying attention to writing styles and word choices.

Cappy had not yet had an article printed, but Asbury Wollums said his writing was going from bad to fair — encouragement enough. Even Willa took an interest in his writing, her job being to count the words and spaces. Counting the spaces was her own idea: "What's left out is oft times as important as what's left in," she said.

Cappy had saved enough money from his job as runner for the paper to buy a secondhand Brownie Kodak. A good clear picture could sometimes take the place of a whole slew of words, he reasoned. One Sunday morning he took his

Kodak and writing tablet in search of a story that he believed Asbury would not throw out.

Turkey white had been building an ark since 1909. It started as a house for his betrothed but he swore on a stack of Baptist Bibles that God told him he was wasting his time nailing together a house unless it would float. Turkey decided to build an ark out of concrete blocks, which he could make in his backyard. Making the blocks would be time-consuming, but he knew the finished product would be indestructible, though bulky.

Tired of waiting, and not sure she wanted to marry a man who was building an ark, his fiancée left town with a traveling osteopath.

The Sunday morning that Cappy chose to interview Turkey White, a short barrel-shaped man with a straggly beard that reached to his belt buckle, he found the old man resting under a buckeye tree, staring up at the ark.

"Morning!" Cappy said as he approached Turkey. "In case you don't recognize me since I've grown up, I'm Cap Giberson, Worthy's boy. I'm after a story to put in the newspaper —"

"What newspaper would that be?"

"The *Democrat-Republican Patriot,* you know, the Carrollton newspaper."

"I've heard of it, though I've never actually saw a copy. So you say you're after a story. Well, I suppose I can oblige you if you ain't in no particular hurry."

"I've got time," Cappy said. He sat on a concrete block and prepared to write.

"I set out to build a house for my intended. She had her heart set on living in a house that nobody had lived in previous — foolish when you think about it, but I was too bereft of reasoning powers at the time to heed the warnings. Anyhow, I had took the team and wagon to town to pick up building goods and was home unloading when God spoke to me. He said, 'Forego the house and build something floatable', His exact words."

"Just how did God tell you?"

"He *boomed* it out, the way you'd expect God to talk. Scared the team a mite."

"How near is your ark to being ready to float?" Cappy asked, making rapid notes.

"Near as I can calculate, things going along as they are, she should be water-ready in another ten years, give or take."

"And where are you planning to put her in?"

"The nearest body of water is the Illinois River. Of course, if things work out like God hinted at, there'll be water aplenty right where she's setting."

"Who are you planning to take with you?"

"Funny you should pose that question, as I was in the midst of totaling up who I'll be taking when you come by. It turns out every last prospect is dead and buried. My folks was on the list, but they've been gone twenty years. There was my dog, Lucky, but I buried him last spring. I thought about taking my chickens so's I'd have eggs and drumsticks to partake of, but I wasn't keen on dealing with chicken shit."

"Did God happen to mention why he was sending another flood? My ma says next time will be by fire."

"He did bring that up. He said to make a flood all He has to do is let it rain, hardly no effort there. But fire ain't so easy to produce in quantity. The truth is, God's tired of dealing with the earth and plans to make things easy on Himself, so long as He gets the job done."

"So you're saying you're likely to be the only one on the ark, human or inhuman?"

"I can't see no other way. But lately I've been thinking in another direction. From the way things is going across the waters, it wouldn't surprise me if one of them German bombs went astray and landed here in Greene County before God gets around to providing a flood. So I'm changing my ark to a bomb shelter."

Cappy snapped a picture of Turkey standing in front of his ark-turned-bomb shelter, smiling.

CAPPY PRESENTED ASBURY WITH THE STORY and picture and waited anxiously for his reaction.

"This isn't the kind of thing we usually print," Asbury said. He read the story again.

"But you told me if I was to write, I should read, and I've been reading the *St. Louis Post Dispatch;* the bus depot sells it Sundays. I read about happenings to people who aren't famous. Regular people. So that's how I happened to think of Turkey White. He's a regular man, but he acts irregular."

"Stories like this are called human interest stories," the editor explained. "I have to admit, the idea intrigues me. The trouble is I don't know if Greene County subscribers will take to something new. They're primarily interested in who went to visit what relative or who got married or buried. Are you sure everything in here is an absolute fact? No plumping up, as you call it?"

"It's the absolute facts except for the part about God setting on a concrete block by the side of the road. I put that in to color it up some. The rest is word for word out of Turkey's mouth."

"I'll tell you what. Remove the added color, clean up your grammar, and maybe there'll be room for your story on the back page."

Cappy's next paycheck was three dollars larger.

Chapter XI

Saturday night after the picture show, the Woosley Twins were sitting in a back booth in Oettle's Tavern.

"If you ask me," Ralph said, "the problem is we're too damned good at what we do. Thieving has became so easy it's lost its fire."

"But if we don't thieve," George said, "how do we fill up our nights?"

The two redheaded pranksters sat not speaking for several minutes, drinking their beers and tapping their fingers to the jukebox.

"I think we've made some mountainous mistakes," Ralph said finally.

"For instance?"

"For instance, the time we stole that fancy silverware from Wiley Roady's house. It wasn't even wrote up in the paper, and you know why? Because Wiley didn't give a shit. All he done was tell his insurance man and he ended up with more money than the silverware was worth in the first place.

"And the time we broke into Franklin Linder's house, we come away from there with a radio and his wife's fur wrap but not a lick of notice."

"That fur wrap was a scary thing," George said. "How Linder's wife could wear a dead fox around her neck puzzles me yet, with them bug eyes staring at the hairs on her chin. And that radio never did play."

"You're missing the point. What I'm getting at is we didn't gain no notice that time either. Thinking has brought me to this," Ralph continued. "The reason thieving has lost its spark is because we're taking from people who don't give a damn. We should start with the widow women. They're great ones for keepsakes."

"But if people start complaining and the sheriff checks deeper, ain't he likely to catch us?"

"You're thinking right up with me now," Ralph said. "We'd be kept on our toes and thievery will get back its fire."

"What would you think of starting with Macel Scroggins?" George asked. "I'll wager she don't carry no insurance, but I can't say for sure if she's a widow. She may be a grass widow, for all I know."

"Macel will be at the picture show Saturday night, she never misses one," Ralph said. "We'll drop by her house and see what she's got hid away."

Macel never bothered to lock her doors, so entering the house was easy. Each twin carried a flashlight. "There sure as hell ain't much of value," George said, rummaging through dresser drawers and closets.

"The idea is to take something *Macel* thinks is of value," Ralph said. "Now what would an old crone like her want to hang on to till her dying day?" He opened the drawers of the sideboard; nothing there except a yellowed tablecloth and napkins, and some dish towels with embroidered nasturtiums in each corner.

"Oh, oh, what have we got here?" He dusted off a picture of a young man in uniform. "It says, 'To Macel from Halbert With Love'. Do you think she could be a real widow after all?"

"Anything's possible," George said. He shone the light on the faded photograph. "We found what we was looking for. We'll take this little momentum and be on our way."

THE FOLLOWING MONDAY AFTER SCHOOL, Cappy rode the bus to Carrollton to ask Sheriff Perdun if any crimes had been committed over the weekend that he could write about. When the sheriff told him of the theft of Macel Scroggins's photo, Cappy saw it as a chance to do Macel, as well as his reporting career, some good. Following Asbury Wollums's advice to go to the source of a story, the next day he went directly to Macel's house from school, pencil and notebook in hand. He found her on her knees, loosening the dirt around a bed of begonias.

"Miss Scroggins? I'm Cap Giberson, Worthy's boy, and I'm here to ask about your troubles. Maybe I can put the story in the newspaper and help find out who did the thievery. That's my job, writing stories for the *Democrat-Republican Patriot*."

Macel looked up. "Oh, I know who did the thievery, but I

doubt there's a way of proving it. Some animals do their pilfering in the dark of the night, and it's the same with them Woosley Twins. They ain't smart, but they don't leave tracks, like the snakes in the grass they are."

"What exactly was stolen?"

Nothing much. Just an old dusty photograph of someone I cared about in my younger days. We was to marry when he got home from the Spanish-American War — but he never got home." She returned to her digging.

After supper, Cappy went to his room and wrote a short item, hoping for Asbury's approval.

THIEVES IN THE NIGHT
by Cappy Giberson

This reporter has just finished talking to Miss Macel Scroggins who was the victim of a crime of stealing last Saturday night while she sat in the picture show watching "Jesse James," *a picture about stealing. The item that the thieves took was not worth much in the way of money, but to Miss Scroggins it was worth the world. If anybody has any idea who might have done this cowardly trick, stop by this newspaper office and you will be given the latest issue of the paper as a reward. And keep your doors and windows locked.*

Asbury studied the article. "Leave out the part about a reward, I don't want to get that started. The warning about locking doors and windows is a service to the readers; that can stay in." He handed the paper to Cappy, and went back to his work.

WHEN RALPH AND GEORGE WOOSLEY READ Cappy's account of the theft, they felt like celebrities. For the first time their work had made the front page. But their elation was short-lived.

"Hold on," George said, "we're no better off than when we was stealing for money instead of fame. The least that old hag could've done was say she *thought* it was us. What if we was to write a letter and not sign it and say something like — rumor has it that two tall red-headed men was seen in the vicin. . . . Shit, Ralph, do you know how to spell that word?"

"We ain't writing no letter saying we was seen hanging around her place," Ralph said. "Do that, and we'll be setting in the jailhouse for keeps. I could use a beer. Let's head for Oettle's."

Chapter XII

One hot summer afternoon in 1941, Pick looked out his store window and noticed a stranger going up and down Main Street tacking posters to telephone poles. He walked around Kid Corner and turned on Mill Street, tacking as he walked. Pick joined Bum and Worthy, who were reading one of the signs.

NED HELVY'S TRAVELING TENT SHOW
MUSIC, JUGGLING, MAGIC,
AMATEUR NIGHT WITH PRIZES
"SAINTLY HYPOCRITES AND SAINTLY SINNERS,"
A PLAY IN THREE ACTS
FEATURING NED HELVY
AND HIS LOVELY LEADING LADY,
GLORIA SOMERSET
ALSO "TEN NIGHTS IN A BARROOM"
IN TOWN ONE WEEK ONLY
CHILDREN 10¢, ADULTS 25¢

"I had a sneaking suspicion they wouldn't come this year," Pick said, smiling with anticipation. "From what I hear, tent shows are about a thing of the past."

"I'll take a good old rag opry over a moving picture show any day of the week," Bum said. "I like seeing actors in the flesh instead of merely seeing a picture of their flesh."

"Damn, but that Gloria Somerset has got the right amount of flesh on her," Pick said, "and it's situated in all the right places!"

"She puts Maizie Plato to shame, and then some," Worthy said.

"I never tire of watching *Ten Nights in a Barroom*," Bum said. "There ain't been a time I didn't learn a lesson from it."

"I'm heading home and letting the family in on the big news," Worthy said. "Willa will have the time of her life counting the days till the tent goes up."

When Cappy heard about the tent show, he walked to the Ozbun farm to tell Beany. He could hear the piano all the way from the road.

As expected, Mrs. Ozbun was not easily persuaded to interrupt Beany. "He's practicing for a recital."

"It won't take long, Mrs. Ozbun."

"The tent show's coming to town next week." Cappy greeted Beany with a playful punch. "Can you do your piano practicing early and ride along? Monday's the first night."

"Sure! But what about Dimple?" Beany knew he was second choice.

"She's busy all week learning new cheers. Are you coming or not?"

"I said I was."

"Be ready by 6:30. Ma wants a front-row seat."

THE PASTURE BEHIND THE BIG TENT was filling up fast, but Worthy found a parking place next to the fence. "Everybody get a move on or we won't find an empty seat."

Once inside the tent, Worthy shoved his way through the crowd until he found a row that wasn't full. Beany went in first, then Cappy and Willa, with Worthy taking the seat on the aisle. When it was time for the bally candy to be sold, Worthy wanted to make sure his raised hand would be the first noticed.

Willa sat expectantly, stiff in her tightest corset, her cheeks dusted white with Lady Esther face powder, a dab of vanilla extract behind each ear.

All nine of the Catholic Steinachers were sitting in the row directly in front of the Gibersons; on Cappy's left were the Shackelfords and their noisy kids. Without looking, Cappy guessed who was sitting in back of him — Shag Kallal and his pa. Old Bert was O.K., but Shag smelled of hog lot, even when he hadn't been near a hog. Since Shag was still helping with the Giberson chores, Cappy felt obligated to give him a quick nod.

At eight o'clock the overhead lights went off. As the stage band finished playing "Jersey Bounce", a lively new tune, a side curtain opened and Ned Helvy stepped into the spotlight. He was a tall blond man with a movie-star face; before making his entrance, he had applied a touch of rouge to his smooth cheeks and full, sensuous lips. Cappy thought he could have passed for a traveling preacher. He made a note in his tablet of that.

Ned went to the piano and began to play; he sang welcoming words to the tune of "You Are My Sunshine", looking over his shoulder and smiling at the audience. When he finished, the curtain opened again and Gloria Somerset glided onto the piano bench. She sat with her back to the keys, her shapely legs crossed. Her short curly hair was the same color as Ned's, and her lips were painted cherry red to match her fingernails; false eyelashes outlined her green eyes. She sang "Just My Bill" in a low breathy voice.

Beany whispered to Cappy, "I'd like to have Ned Helvy's job. I'll bet he makes a barrel of money."

The show opened with a pair of knife jugglers, followed by a magician and his girl assistant. The magician's finale was to saw his assistant in half; Cappy was skeptical of the aging magician's skill with a saw. The crowd moaned when the blade divided her body into two wiggling parts, and cheered when she was made whole — Cappy along with them.

The main curtain opened to reveal a parlor, the set for *Saintly Hypocrites and Saintly Sinners.* The magician played the cruel landlord, Gloria Somerset the innocent girl he lured, and Ned Helvy the stranger who saved her from the landlord's clutches. Cappy booed and cheered with the rest of the audience.

After the last act of the play, Ned stepped in front of the curtain carrying a tray filled with bally candy. "Friends and neighbors," he said, waving a small box, "this is not the best saltwater taffy in the world, but it *is* the best saltwater taffy for sale tonight!" Everyone applauded and cheered.

The bally candy was sold quickly. Ned Helvy remained. "Well, neighbors, I hope you've had a good time and that you'll come back every night. Tomorrow we'll be doing *Ten Nights in a Barroom*. Thursday night will be Amateur Night. And friends, I wouldn't want you to leave without taking along some wisdom I've picked up traveling across this wonderful land of ours. Three words to live by. Loving. Forgiving. Helping. Let's examine them closer."

Cappy was suddenly suspicious. Ned Helvy was beginning to sound like the Reverend Art. The tent show was beginning to sound a lot like a tent revival.

"Loving," Ned continued. "It's easy to love a person who's lovable, but what about the bum on Skid Row? Forgiving. It's not hard to forgive somebody who steps on your toe, but what about forgiving the man who runs off with your wife while you're trying to earn a decent living?

"Now here's a word I want to pass along to you. Philanthropist. Don't let that fancy word scare you, it only means somebody who helps others. Helping may mean bending your back for somebody down on their luck, or offering a helping hand to someone mired in the quicksand of drink, or using one of your God-given talents as a flashlight to light the way out of the dark swamp of life."

Cappy was writing as fast as he could; the word "philanthropist" had piqued his interest. This must be how Tick had felt when he got the call to preach, Cappy thought, as the show ended in a flurry of singing and dancing.

DRIVING HOME, Worthy said, "That Ned Helvy puts on one hell of a show, and he didn't miss a lick on that piano. I'm for going again, Willa."

"We'll go," Cappy said from the back seat, speaking for Beany.

"You weren't provoked into running away with this tent show, were you, Cappy?" Willa asked.

"No, but I got an idea or two."

AFTER THE TENT SHOW, Cappy could not forget the admonition that Ned Helvy hammered home each night — to help others. Soon the opportunity presented itself.

Ollie Beechum, eighty years old, was a new widow, bringing the number of Old Kane widows to forty-three. The day her late husband's small railroad pension arrived, Ollie would go from the post office to Pick's Store to exchange the check for cash — eleven ones, twenty quarters, fifty dimes, thirty nickels, forty-five pennies — out of which she paid the light bill, her weekly life insurance premium and church tithe, bought coal for the cookstove, washing powder and blueing for the washtub, and staples for the pantry. The remaining fifteen cents went into an old purse for emergencies such as cough syrup or a new pair of stockings. If she could get through the winter without catching the grippe, the cough syrup money would buy a sack of horehound candy the following spring.

During the summer months, Ollie relied heavily on her garden, and she cold-packed corn, peas and string beans to last the winter. In the cool of the day she would gather dandelion blossoms and bring them into the kitchen, quickly dousing them in cold water to keep them from closing up. Fried crisp, they made a tasty dinner.

Monday mornings Ollie would start a soup pot. The bulk of soup makings she found in the alley behind Pick's Store: lettuce too brown to sell, an occasional soft carrot, sometimes a discarded rib cage of beef.

One beautiful August morning Cappy and Ollie exchanged friendly waves. Cappy noticed her wave was not as hearty as usual; in truth, she had slept crooked on her waving arm and it was feeling stiff, but to Cappy it meant only one thing. Ollie Beechum was beginning to fail. Cappy decided that Ollie was that long-awaited opportunity to do good.

So, Cappy began walking through the countryside in search of Good Samaritans. He met a couple of Worthy's friends on their way to Macoupin Creek to fish. When Cappy told them of Ollie's narrow circumstances and failing health, they offered to cut her grass and weed. "If she wants to give you a few pennies, don't argue," Cappy reminded them.

He flagged down Bum Hetzel driving his daughters to Sunday School. Bum agreed to haul away Ollie's trash, as he was always looking for anything that would burn. (Once a year, he built a big bonfire of his trash and had the neighbors in for a pig roast.) "Don't be surprised if she hands you a dime," Cappy said to Bum.

The Wednesday Afternoon Missionary Society was dedicated to bettering the lives of the heathen natives in Africa. The good Christian ladies spent hours studying pictures of the sober, naked, dark-skinned men and women, deciding which article of clothing would benefit them. Once Cappy told them of Ollie Beechum's plight, they put aside three cotton dresses for *her* benefit.

A cigar box to hold contributions for Ollie sat on the bar in Oettle's Tavern, the one place Ollie was sure not to set foot in. And Wiley Roady, owner of the ball bat factory, gave $50 to the Beechum Fund, listing it among his other charitable contributions. By the end of the month, the grand total raised was $110.56.

OLLIE BEECHUM WINS DRAWING

Ollie Beechum, well-known widow of Henry Beechum, was the winner of a recent Oddfellows drawing. The prize was $110.56 and three everyday dresses. It was Mrs. Beechum's lucky day.

Early Saturday morning, Cappy stopped by Ollie's. He was prepared to engage in a little storytelling, knowing she would not accept help without giving something in return. He could hear her out back chopping wood. Before long she won't have to work like a horse, he thought.

"Afternoon, Miss Ollie," he said cheerily.

"Afternoon back to you," she said, her eyes bright.

"I hope I'm not bothering you, but there's a matter of import to take up."

"I'm glad for the reason to rest," she said, leaning her ax against a tree. Her face dripped sweat; she wiped her cheeks and forehead with her apron before speaking. "What's on your mind this hot day?"

"This," Cappy said, handing her the sack of dresses and the envelope of money. "You won the Oddfellows drawing last Saturday night, first prize was $110.56 and three everyday dresses."

Ollie looked at the money, the most she had seen in one lump. "I don't remember buying a drawing chance. My mind must've been off on a trip," she said, puzzled. "But forgetting's to be expected, the age I'm at. I won't know how to act being rich."

"I'll be going," said Cappy, happy to see Ollie smiling, the reward Ned Helvy must have meant, "but I'll stop in now and then to see how you're getting along." When he left, she was still looking at the money and shaking her head in disbelief.

ONE MORNING THE NEXT MONTH, Cappy stopped to see Ollie. Her grass was cut, zinnias and marigolds were still blooming, and not one dandelion could be found in the yard. The garden plot had been turned back into pasture, grown naturally high with thistles and jimsonweeds. Cappy found the old woman sitting inside her small house picking at a raveling on her dress.

"Morning, Miss Ollie," Cappy said. "Are you doing better these days?"

"Better than what?" she said in a surly tone.

"Since your good luck. Aren't Pa's friends working to please you?"

"Oh, I'm near pleased to death. I can't look up but what them friends of Worthy's are under foot. And I can't step out of the house for so much as a breath of air that they ain't shoving me back inside, afraid I'll tire myself. I ain't had a mess of dandelions since they started coming, with them bound and determined to dig up every last plant!"

When Cappy left, Ollie was rolling lint into a ball. "And them three everyday dresses hang on me like a sack!" she called after him.

It was clear to Cappy that his good intentions had missed their mark. He had to put the matter straight before Ollie died of boredom.

ODDFELLOWS' MISTAKE

It has been learned that Ollie Beechum, widow of Henry Beechum, did not win first prize in the recent Oddfellows drawing as announced. The Oddfellows are sorry for the mistake, and are asking Mrs. Beechum to return what is left of the prize money. She can keep the dresses.

Ollie put on her sunbonnet and set to work. Two spindly dandelion plants had miraculously escaped the hoe; she pumped a tin of rainwater from the cistern and lovingly sprinkled each plant.

Her step light, she walked to the post office to pick up last month's pension. Pick exchanged bills and coins for the check, while she looked longingly at the bin of horehound candy. She went home and started a pot of soup.

Chapter XIII

⤙

The day began like any Sunday. By seven o'clock Worthy had killed, scalded, and plucked a roasting hen, and Willa had an angel food cake baking in the oven. They weren't expecting company for Sunday dinner, but if some showed up unexpectedly, they would not be embarrassed.

Willa had stopped attending church because it reminded her of how Tick had left home two years earlier. But she listened faithfully to Theo Jones' "Radio Church" broadcast every Sunday from El Paso, Texas. When she had a dollar to spare, she sent it to Brother Jones, for without support from listeners his ministry could not continue. He made that clear several times during each broadcast.

As Brother Jones was offering the closing prayer, an agitated voice said, "We interrupt this broadcast —" followed by the voice of President Roosevelt. Worthy and Willa dropped what they were doing and leaned close to their radio, trying to comprehend the president's somber words about a bombing somewhere. Cappy listened to President Roosevelt's calm voice. He didn't sound worried, but maybe he was hiding his true feelings to keep from causing panic across the country. The baked chicken and angel food cake sat untouched.

Cappy could hear his folks talking quietly throughout the night. Once it sounded like Willa was crying. In the morning, though, they went about their chores as if it were an ordinary December 8.

A makeshift enlistment office was set up in the courthouse. When the doors opened, Worthy and Cappy were first in a long line waiting to enlist. Boys a couple of years older than Cappy laughed and joked as if they were about to enter the fun house at the county fair.

Willa waited at home, counting the steady ticks of the mantel clock that sounded around the empty house. She envisioned a day when there would be no more Gibersons to count. But her worries were unwarranted. Worthy was too old, the recruiter said, and Cappy too young. If the war was still in progress, Cappy could try again in a couple of years, but unless the country was in a dire pinch, Worthy could remain on the farm indefinitely.

EVEN THOUGH IT WAS THE MIDDLE OF THE SCHOOL YEAR, Dimple abruptly moved back to Alton with her parents — their marriage difficulties settled. Cappy was sad but somewhat relieved to see her go. If he intended to follow Asbury Wollums's advice about going to college, he needed to save his money. And, he might have to delay college until he came back from fighting the war.

Beany was as relieved as Cappy to see Dimple leave. Now they could go back to the way things used to be; sitting together in the picture show, going to Mundy's afterward for a hamburger sandwich, watching the girls on Kid Corner. Both boys agreed that Dimple had put a serious strain on their friendship.

"YOU'LL NEVER GUESS WHAT I HEARD on the radio today," Worthy said as he filled his plate. "Somebody high up has took 'Gangbusters' off the air. And do you know why? They say the average man, that's me, will turn to crime from listening to it. Did you ever hear anything so farfetched?"

Cappy broke into the conversation, pointing at a copy of the *Democrat-Republican Patriot*. "Here's something about the war. It says 'Because of high rent, thousands of people are living in tents and tar-paper cities, vacant barns, warehouses, even chicken coops'. Looks like we're lucky to live in a house."

"There's no two ways about it," Worthy said, as if he hadn't heard. "1941 has proved a disappointing year."

Chapter XIV

⌒

Early in 1942, the Selective Service was in full operation. Single men between eighteen and thirty-five, and married men between eighteen and twenty-six, were being called as fast as the draft board could handle the paperwork. The first time a trainload of draftees was scheduled to leave for basic training at Camp Ellis, Illinois, Cappy was at the depot with his Kodak, catching tearful mothers and wives on film saying goodbye to the soon-to-be soldiers. Two of the Steinachers' sons were in that initial group. At the parents' request, the Catholic priest from Jerseyville was there to bless the boys. Cappy snapped a picture of the scene.

CONVERSATIONS IN PICK'S STORE centered around the war and the draft, with speculation on who would be the first casualty.

"I heard the Woosley Twins was called up but couldn't make the grade because of flat feet," Worthy said. "If you ask me, they'd make fine targets. While the enemy was aiming at them, the rest of their outfit could be invading the beaches safe."

"What about Drayton Hunt?" Pick asked. "He likes a fracas so much, let him put on a uniform and fracas with the big boys."

"The bastard's too old," Worthy said. "He must be over 40 by now." He hated the man as intensely as on the day of Chastity's funeral.

"Maybe if you was to slip some money under the table at the draft board, Hunt's name would go to the top of the list, old or not!" Bum said.

"Don't tempt me!" Worthy, as well as every other man around Old Kane, knew Drayton Hunt as a troublemaker going back to when he was a boy.

As A CHILD, Drayton had lived with his mother, Mae, and his little sister in a house near Ingram's Dump. He never knew who his father was. He watched men come and go, making brief boisterous stops at his mother's bedroom, pressing coins in her hand on their way out, promising to return. He wondered whether his father ever came.

Still, in his youthful eyes, Mae Hunt — with her black, marcelled hair, and rouged lips — was the most beautiful woman in the world. Mae, concerned with putting food on the table and coal in the stove, gave little thought to her children, least of all to her homely, adoring son.

When Drayton was ten, he started pulling legs from crawling bugs and wings from butterflies. Then he went on to bigger game: Mae's chickens. He would tie a rock to an old hen's leg and toss her into Macoupin Creek, timing how long it took her to sink out of sight. The chicken that survived the longest was a large Rhode Island Red rooster, which thrashed around in the cold creek water a minute and fifty-four seconds before going under.

His sister had been nine when Drayton began slipping into her bedroom at night, once or twice a week. At first he only cuddled and stroked her smooth little body, but after some coaxing she allowed him to ease a finger in between her legs.

On her eleventh birthday, Drayton decided his sister could take the real thing. He placed a pillow beneath her thin hips to put her within easier reach, and climbed into the narrow bed. Without prompting, she opened her legs to him, as demurely as a lady opening a Japanese fan. From then on, he visited her bed every night. On wash day, when Mae noticed bloodstains on the pillow, she assumed her daughter had suffered a nosebleed.

I may not be no Charles Boyer, Drayton thought, but I know how to get the most out of a female.

Now, ON A HOT JULY AFTERNOON IN 1942, Drayton stopped by Oettle's Tavern to cool off. He noticed the Woosley Twins sitting in a booth near the back door. Over the years, he had been watching Ralph and George, mildly amused at their pranks. All these boys need is some guidance by the old master, he thought.

"Hey, Buck, bring me a beer, and snap to it!" He took the seat opposite the twins, who always sat on the same side of the booth. Buck hobbled over with a bottle of warm beer;

Drayton took a long swig before speaking. "Well, now, what've you two good-looking fellas been up to?"

Ralph and George felt proud at being noticed by Drayton Hunt. To them, he was not a troublemaker, but smart and a snappy dresser.

"A little here, a little there," Ralph said. "We ain't in your league, Drayton."

"You could be with a little coaching. How about you boys meeting me tonight and we'll see what fun we can find? Better yet, I'll pick you up about seven in my Moon and we'll take it from there."

"I sure do admire that Moon of yours," George said, happy at the thought of riding in the shiny blue car.

"Well, tonight you can see her up close, but make sure you change out of them dirty overhalls first."

"We'll be clean as if it was a Saturday night," George promised.

"Well, boys, I hate to drink and run," Drayton said, as he finished his beer, "but I've got other holes to dig, as the saying goes."

Drayton was on time to meet the twins who had been waiting by the mailbox for an hour. Ralph climbed into the front seat, George the back. Drayton took the Moon through its gears and turned toward Old Kane. He drove all the way through town, and back into the country. The twins were in hog heaven.

"You know, there ain't a time I pass this way without thinking of that little blondie girl of Worthy's that died," Ralph said, as they approached the Giberson farm. "Georgieboy here wanted some of her dew, but she wasn't interested."

"She was in this very car back when I first bought it," Drayton said. "Her little butt was setting on the very seat where your big butt's setting, Ralph. Like they say, it's a small world."

Hardly a day went by that Drayton didn't think back to 1924 and how he had first met Chastity Giberson. He had given her a ride in his motor car — a Moon that he had gone to St. Louis to buy and that had put him forever in debt. It had been raining, he remembered, and he was proud she allowed him to pick her up. Her figure had been blossoming and her hair was long and golden. She was the most beautiful woman he had ever seen, even though he suspected she had barely entered her teens. At twenty-three, Drayton had not been much to look at, but he had wooed Chastity with his new car. He could still see her beside him, caressing the soft blue cushions of the Moon with her slender fingers.

Drayton still had the Moon, almost as good as new eighteen years later. If I had it to do over, I'd of done things different, he thought, as he crossed Macoupin Creek Bridge with the Woosley Twins. Drayton had never told anyone about his final encounter with Chastity Giberson, not even to brag to the twins. He liked carrying the secret memory to recall when he was feeling lonely. Drayton turned down a narrow, dark road and stopped at a heavy iron gate. He took a flashlight from the glove box and climbed out of the car, unsure why he had come to this desolate place.

"Here we are, boys, Jalappa Cemetery." He switched on his flashlight and led the way across several family plots, weaving in and out among the familiar headstones. He stopped when he came to a large stone with "Giberson" etched in tall letters. Worthy Giberson, Senior, and his wife Nellie were buried on half the plot, along with their three infants. In the southeast corner a small stone reading "Chastity" lay by itself. Drayton's first emotion of longing was immediately replaced by implacable hatred — for Worthy, the man who stood between him and his son. As if Worthy were beside him to see his daughter defiled, Drayton unbuttoned his pants and managed a trickle of yellow water running over her name.

"You boys care to join me?" Drayton asked.

"I don't have to pee, but I sure as hell need to shit," George said, his desire to please Drayton overwhelming. He pulled down his pants and squatted.

"Jesus Christ, hold off till we get out of firing range!" Drayton said, as he and Ralph quickly backed away.

George wiped himself with a leaf from the peony bush that decorated Chastity's grave.

Chapter XV

Of all the changes brought about by World War II, nothing raised the ire of Old Kane more than the introduction of Daylight Saving Time, known as "Roosevelt's Time". Brother Beams set the tone by announcing that the Old Kane Baptist Church would remain on "God's Time", resulting in half the worshipers arriving an hour early each Sunday, the other half as church was letting out.

Roosevelt's Time caused serious rifts around town, with Pick's Store the scene of daily debates.

"The way I see it, the entire United States is out of kilter," Pick said as he poured coffee for his regulars. "You've got Jerseyville running on Roosevelt's Time and Carrollton on God's Time. If the war don't drive a man crazy, trying to figure out the time of day will."

"Here's how I handle the clock," Worthy said. "When the cock crows, I haul out of bed, and when the sun goes down I haul back in. That ain't so hard."

"I like to ruined my good watch, setting it up and back," Bum said. "It's stowed away in my damned sock drawer till the kafewgulty is over and done with."

"Roosevelt's Time has sure played hash with Willa's counting," Worthy said. "She's forever studying the mantel clock trying to figure out where that hour went."

"Have you all heard about Charlie Turner's girl joining the Army?" Worthy asked, after a pause.

"It's a blessing Charlie ain't alive to live down that heartache," Bum said.

"Women in the Army are a coming thing," Pick said, showing the men a headline in the *St. Louis Post Dispatch*. "They say women all ages are flocking to join."

"Women acting like men!" Worthy scoffed. "It's getting so you can't walk down the damned street without meeting a woman wearing men's trousers."

"Sorry, boys, but this is all of the coffee." Pick divided the last drops among the cups.

"Jesus, I bet Roosevelt never runs out of coffee," Bum said. He usually drank about eight cups a day before rationing.

"Being president has its privileges else they'd never find anybody to take the job," Worthy said. He couldn't imagine, however, what those privileges might be.

"He likely drinks tea, anyway. Coffee's for the everyday working man," Bum said.

"I hate to be the bearer of more bad news", Pick said, "but sugar's joined the ration list. We'd all better learn to curb our sweet tooth."

"It ain't only foodstuffs," Worthy chimed in. "Finice Darr at the garage says gasoline rationing is coming fast. Us farmers will fare better than most, but Finice says if you live in town you'll have to get by on four gallons a week. And if you have to call long distance to Jerseyville, you're rationed to five minutes of talking." He seldom, if ever, called Jerseyville.

Pick sensed it was time to guide the conversation away from the war. He couldn't decide whether to ask about Worthy's bad back or Worthy's boy. So, he took a deep breath and asked, "Say, Worthy, how's Cappy doing at the newspaper?" "Damned if he doesn't come up with stories worth reading."

"Cappy's on his way up in this world. I taught him everything he knows about storytelling, and it's paying off handsome. My only grief is he's bent on writing them down instead of telling them."

"What do you hear from that other boy of yours," Pick asked, "the one that took off with the traveling preacher?"

"Not a single solitary word," Worthy said, "but I expect he'll come home some day — sadder but wiser." It had been three years since Tick had left home.

"Is it true he's in the healing business?" Pick asked.

"I don't know nothing about his business," Worthy snapped. Discussing Tick made him edgy. Would he ever see Tick again?

"I was thinking maybe he could give some relief to your bad back, so we could get some relief from your bellyaching," Pick replied. He knew how to get Worthy's goat.

In JUNE, Cappy graduated from Old Kane High School, finishing with high marks. Giving incorrect answers had long since lost its sport, although he still believed a well-placed piece of storying could be to his advantage. His Freshman English teacher, Mr. Berry, had been quick to recognize his talent for writing. As a way of challenging him to improve, Mr. Berry began assigning extra writing — short stories to be read aloud once a month at the Friday assemblies.

The day after Cappy received his diploma, he tried again to enlist, but was turned down because he lived on a farm.

"But I only help out on the farm in my spare time," Cappy insisted, as he faced the recruiting sergeant. "Mostly I work at the newspaper."

"Don't matter," the sergeant said. "If we take you, we'll have to take all the farm boys, and we'll be in deep shit from the higher-ups. Besides that you're only seventeen. Next!"

Beany Ozbun, already eighteen, would have been eligible for a farm deferment, too, but a week before graduation from high school his mother insisted that the family move to town where she said the air was not so "heavy".

"I wish I was going with you," Cappy said to Beany, meaning it. "Your folks picked a poor time to sell the farm."

"I'll tell you what. When the war's over, I'll come home covered with medals for my heroic escapades, and you can write a book about me. We'll both be famous."

"You've got it!" Cappy said, with more enthusiasm than he felt. He tried to envision his life without Beany. No more movies or swimming in Macoupin Creek or discussing plans for the future. But with the way things were going, Cappy thought, there might not be a future.

The morning Beany was to leave for basic training, only his father and Cappy were at the train depot to wave him off.

His mother, Viola, had taken to her bed with heart flutters. While the three were standing around, Cappy tried to think of something to lighten the moment, a joke, or the recollection of a funny movie he and Beany had seen together, but it was no use. Beany had a forced smile on his face, and Cappy swallowed hard a few times. Beany's father shook his son's hand, then quickly turned away.

The whistle signaled that the train was about to leave. "Well, Cappy, this looks like it," Beany said. "I'll send letters when I get a chance. Just don't fall in the creek and drown while I'm gone."

"And don't you follow a tire track off and get lost." Cappy gave his friend a bear hug. He watched until the caboose was out of sight, and then he walked to the highway to await the next bus to Carrollton. It was time to ask Asbury Wollums for a full-time job.

"COME ON IN, CAPPY, but I've only got a minute," the overworked editor said. He had already lost two employees to the draft.

"A minute's all I want. I know you told me I should get some college before I can be a reporter, and I'm already saving up my money, but I wouldn't feel right going with the war on. So if I promise to get more schooling after the war, can I bypass it for the time being and work here every day?"

Although Asbury was reluctant to admit it, Cappy's stories *were* helping sell newspapers. The boy had a gift for ferreting stories from people before they knew what was happening, and making them feel good about it.

"We can give it a try," he said, desperate. "Starting Monday, you can be on the payroll full time. The pay isn't much, and it will be on a trial basis."

"I've got some ideas for changes, like spelling you with the editorials. You'd be getting a rest and I could speak my mind. What do you say?"

"It's good you have ambition, Cappy, but nobody starts at the top," the editor replied. He admired the boy's gumption, but had to laugh at his ego. "What I had in mind was putting you in charge of coordinating news from Old Kane and around. Mrs. Biesemeyer collects news from Old Kane proper, Ollie Beechum from east and west of town, Mrs. Steinacher from north and south. Sometimes the good ladies stray into each other's territory and the same item may appear more than once. Your job is to see that doesn't happen. Keep track of whatever you spend on bus fare, and I'll see you're reimbursed the end of each week."

"Is that my only job?" Cappy was crestfallen, his seventeen-year-old pride wounded.

"You'll also be in charge of reporting on new babies born in Greene County, getting names, weights, those kinds of things. Check the list of births at the hospital every day and go from there. If you have any questions, ask my wife, Min. She'll be assisting me until the war's over." Not exactly what I had in mind, Cappy thought, but it was a start.

CAPPY ARRIVED EARLY FOR HIS FIRST DAY of full-time work. Although excited with the prospect of working for the newspaper, he was not looking forward to answering to Asbury's wife, who had also become a war-time fill-in.

Min Wollums appeared the same age as Asbury, in her mid-thirties, but she weighed nearly two hundred pounds. She usually wore the highest heeled shoes Cappy had ever seen, teetering precariously at the bus depot while buying a magazine or cigarettes. Her hair was silver from bleach, "platinum" it was called, he later learned. With silk stockings rationed, the only types available were cotton or rayon, and Min refused to be seen wearing "old ladies' stockings". After every bath, she carefully penciled seam lines down the back of her bare legs.

"So you're the Cappy Giberson I've heard so much about," Min said, looking him over as he stood in front of her: a tall, gangly boy with short blond hair that wouldn't lie down, and the beginning of a pale moustache above his lip. His pants and shirt, both heavily starched, were neatly ironed.

"Az tells me you're smart but unseasoned, so my job is to season you up a bit." She continued looking straight at him, causing him to blush. "You know, Cappy, I have a feeling we'll get along famously." She smiled warmly, and ruffled his hair. Cappy smiled back; he was embarrassed, but what else could he do?

"Now, then, let's get down to business. According to Az, you're to handle birth announcements. You can get a list at the hospital. Just make sure you don't knock on some housewife's door too early. A woman doesn't like to answer the door before she puts her face on." Without waiting for a response, she turned to her own duties. Cappy caught a scent of heavy perfume.

CAPPY WALKED TO THE HOSPITAL and looked at the list of new babies. Only two had been born the month of June, both from Old Kane. The list was nearly four weeks old — a new job and already he was a month behind.

It was 10:00 A.M. when he walked to the Margeson house. He hoped he had allowed time for the new mother to apply her face.

Mary Lee Margeson was sitting on the back step stemming strawberries. Her face was bare of any makeup.

"My baby's sound asleep," Mary Lee said, as she put a large ripe strawberry in Cappy's mouth. "She's such a good baby. She never cries, not even at night."

"What's her name?"

"Sarah Jane, after my granny. Are you planning to tell all about my baby for the newspaper? That would be nice for her scrapbook."

"I'm supposed to write how much she weighs and her name, things like that. And I'm supposed to look at every baby — that's my own idea. I was thinking it might be good to put in the announcement if the baby is pretty." Cappy was pleased with how professional he sounded.

"She's asleep in her basket, but you're welcome to see her. Sarah Jane's a little doll, if you don't mind a mother bragging some."

The mother led the way into the house, through the kitchen piled high with dirty dishes, and upstairs to the nursery. The entire house smelled of last night's liver and onions. Except for a night-light in the shape of a teddy bear, the nursery was dark; the shades were drawn to the windowsills. Mary Lee turned on a small table lamp.

As Cappy approached the basket, the proud mother pulled back the covers. The lamp didn't offer much light; Cappy could barely make out the tiny face.

"She's awake," Cappy said, as he leaned closer. "Her eyes are wide open."

"They're always open, even when she's fast asleep. Babies do that until they're about six-months old, you know. I expect by Christmas she'll be closing them. Here, would you like to hold her?" Before Cappy could object, the mother had lifted the baby from the crib. "Just be careful and not drop her."

"This is the first baby I ever held," he said, holding the infant gingerly. "I expected her to be doing a lot of squirming around, but she's still as a post." He looked into the blue, painted eyes.

"She never cries, she's such a good baby," Mary Lee said again. She took the small bundle from Cappy and began to rock from side to side, humming softly.

"I need to be getting back to Carrollton," Cappy said. "Thanks for letting me see Sarah Jane." By the time the bus pulled into the depot, Cappy had worked himself into a rage.

Asbury was proofing some copy when Cappy returned. "How's your first day going?"

"How come you didn't tell me about the Margeson baby being a play baby? I felt like a ninny standing there holding a doll!"

"I assumed you knew it, the story was all over town. The baby, a girl I believe, lived a week, one of those babies born with a large head. The day Mrs. Margeson came home from the hospital, she called the dime store and had them send one of those dolls that drinks and wets. She carries it with her wherever she goes. A sad case."

Cappy sat at his desk and stared at the blank piece of paper. He knew what he had to write.

Bob and Mary Lee Margeson have a baby girl named Sarah Jane after Mary's granny. She weighs six pounds and never fusses like most new babies. Her beautiful bright blue eyes are wide open so she doesn't miss a thing. Bob and Mary Lee are very proud of Sarah Jane. Grandparents are Mr. and Mrs. Pete Margeson and Mr. and Mrs. Lloyd Winters.

When Asbury saw what Cappy had written, he yelled, "You know I can't allow this to be printed about the Margeson baby. How many times do I have to tell you, news has to be the truth!"

"It's the truth as far as Mary Lee Margeson knows it. I did it so she'd have a clipping for her baby's scrapbook. I made her a promise." Everything can't go by rules, Cappy thought, even news.

"Either you keep that imagination under control, or I'll hire someone else. But this is an abnormal circumstance," the editor said, softening his tone. "I'll allow your announcement to be printed as written. This time."

Cappy pictured Mary Lee Margeson proudly clipping out the announcement and pasting it in Sarah Jane's scrapbook.

Cappy's first letter from beany was good news.

Dear Cap, They took one look at me and said the country would be bet-
ter off if I'm playing the piano instead of carrying a gun! I'm going into
something called "Special Services" and all of the guys will be putting
shows together to entertain the soldiers who have to fight. When we
aren't in a show we have to wear uniforms and follow the rules like
everybody else. I told you that piano practicing would pay off. Be sure
and let me know when your storytelling does as well.

Your pal,
Beany

Cappy immediately answered. He missed Beany even
more than Tick.

Congratulations on dodging the fighting. So that you don't waste your
time feeling sorry for me, I now have a job at Asbury Wollums's news-
paper. Next time I write I'll tell you all about it. I may not be getting
applause, but I am getting pay, and they let me wear any kind of clothes
I want.

Your literary pal,
Cappy

Chapter XVI

Willie Biesemeyer was the first Greene County boy to come home from the war in a box. A soldier, Willie's close friend since basic training, had been sent along to accompany the body; at Mrs. Biesemeyer's insistence, he moved in until the funeral, sleeping upstairs in Willie's bed beneath Willie's high school banners, tossing Willie's old basketball through a hoop hanging on the wall. Willie himself was on display downstairs in the front parlor wearing his dress uniform, a dress hat at rest in his folded hands.

The initial preparation of Willie's body had been done by the Army — embalming and concealing the fatal wound — leaving Franklin Linder, the local undertaker, to dress the body and apply pancake makeup and rouge. But Franklin was not at all satisfied with the sloppy attention to detail by the Army embalmers. With a small scalpel he removed the sutures from the carotid incisions and redid the work, fashioning tiny even stitches on each side of Willie's neck. The fussiest quilter in the Old Kane Quilting Society could not surpass Franklin's meticulous stitching.

As with every male corpse that came to his establishment, Franklin examined the penis. This was the smallest he had seen in a lifetime of embalming, smaller than his smallest finger. Before dressing the body, he set up a row of bright lights and took a picture to add to his collection. On a slack day, he liked to spread the pictures on the embalming table and test his ability to name each corpse from that isolated bit of anatomy.

ASBURY CALLED CAPPY INTO HIS OFFICE. "I suppose you've heard about the Biesemeyer boy — a sad thing but bound to happen sooner or later," he said, as if it were just another news item. "The body's at the family home and I want you to show up tonight at the wake. There's a soldier who came with the body, you might want to talk to him, you know, find out the circumstances of Willie's death, whatever's pertinent. And pay attention to anything he says that might add color, personal facts such as, did he have a girl waiting somewhere? Was he proud to be serving his country? You know what I want, readers eat that stuff up. But make sure you stick to the facts."

Cappy could not help but think of Beany as he left for the dreaded assignment. While he still doubted there was a God, else the world would not be in such a state, sometimes he caught himself asking God to watch over his best friend. It was too bad about Willie Biesemeyer, but he was glad it wasn't Beany.

The Biesemeyers' small parlor, lined with folding chairs, was filled with sweet-smelling gardenias. An American flag was draped over the lower half of the gunmetal-gray coffin, and a large spray of red roses with a ribbon that said *Our Son* partially covered the flag. Mr. and Mrs. Biesemeyer stood close by the bier, shaking hands, their faces set in smiles as if they were welcoming guests to a Christmas party. Jerry Wayham, the soldier friend, stood solemnly at the foot of the coffin, legs slightly apart, one hand resting on the butt of his rifle, his other hand behind his back.

When, in spite of the bitter cold November evening, Jerry Wayham went outside to smoke, Cappy pulled up the collar of his coat and followed. He found the soldier standing next to the garage trying to light his cigarette in the brisk wind.

"My name's Cappy Giberson," he said, as he approached the soldier who looked no older than himself. Cappy started to hold out his hand, but he wasn't sure soldiers were allowed to shake hands with civilians.

"Jerry Wayham." The soldier offered his own hand.

"I work for the *Democrat-Republican Patriot*," Cappy said, "and I'm supposed to write a news story about Willie. We were fairly close neighbors, but he was older than me. What I remember most about him was how he and his brothers painted everything on their farm yellow. It was a sight to see."

"I know, Willie told me that story. He said he was barely old enough to hold a paint brush. We had a good laugh over it." A quick smile crossed the soldier's face.

"Being the first war hero from Old Kane, people will

want to know how he came to die and any personal things you could tell about him."

Jerry took several draws on his cigarette before he answered. "I guess that's reasonable. What exactly do you want to know?"

"Did he have a girlfriend waiting somewhere? How did he die? Those kinds of things."

Jerry took a deep breath, inhaling the smoke. "Willie and I were with the invasion forces that landed in Africa, not far from Casablanca. We soon ran up against the enemy, November 8th I think it was, but in three or four days the skirmish was over —"

"Slow down a little," Cappy interrupted. "I don't want to miss anything." He thought that this time he'd have a story Asbury would approve of.

"O. K. Well, our company was heading back to our quarters when a sniper up in a tree started taking potshots. Half-a-dozen men got wounded. I've never seen Willie any madder than he was that day."

"And that's when it happened?"

"No," Jerry said. "Willie started firing at that tree and didn't stop until the sniper fell to the ground dead. More of us would have died if he hadn't got that sniper when he did."

"He was a hero, all right. His folks will be proud when they read this."

"Willie was a hero, but not only for shooting a sniper. That first night back in camp, we went to the bar to celebrate — actually it was a small tent where you could get a beer and sit and smoke or play cards. Willie ordered for both of us, and that was the start of the trouble. The guy behind the bar handed him one bottle and said, 'Here's your beer, but your pal will have to stay thirsty. We don't serve queers.' Am I going too fast?" he asked Cappy.

"You're O.K. so far." Though surprised at Jerry Wayham's story, Cappy concentrated on his writing, hoping his face was impassive.

"Willie let go with a punch to the guy's nose, and then five or six of his buddies jumped the both of us. Before the air cleared, Willie had taken a knife in the back. It must have gone directly into his lung. In a few minutes he was dead. When those goons realized what they'd done, they took off running."

"Did you know the one with the knife?"

"No, they were all from another outfit."

"How come the guy tending bar made that crack about you being a queer?"

Jerry hesitated briefly. "Because I am." Defiantly, he stared at Cappy.

Cappy put down his pencil. "And Willie didn't care?"

"He was the same as me."

Cappy recalled that long-ago summer day when he and Beany had experimented with each other. "Did you tell this to his folks?" Cappy asked.

"I've never told a soul. As far as they know, he was killed by a sniper, and the Army brass sure didn't want the real story to get out."

"How'd you come to tell me — a stranger?"

"I had to unload my guts before they exploded, and you happened to be in the right place at the right time. What I said isn't for your paper, I guess you know that." He put out his cigarette. "I'd better go back inside. I don't like leaving Willie alone."

CAPPY WROTE A TWO-COLUMN ACCOUNT of Willie's life for the paper, and under his picture was the following caption:

DEATH OF A WAR HERO

Willie Biesemeyer, Old Kane's first war hero, is pictured above wearing the dress uniform of his country. While fighting in Africa, he single-handedly wiped out a den of snipers without thinking of his own safety. He paid with his life. Old Kane is proud of its hero, Willie Biesemeyer. Funeral services will be Saturday at the Baptist Church.

Asbury printed the photograph and article on the front page of the paper, having no reason to doubt that every word was factual.

Cappy wrote a letter to Beany.

I hope you're taking care of yourself, Old Bean. Watch your back while you're sitting at the piano. You never know when some guy with a knife will get p.o.'d at the song you're playing. When you get home we'll —

THE SCHOOL YEAR WAS COMING TO A CLOSE. Little by little Margaret Self had been cleaning out her desk drawers, deciding between things to keep and things to throw away. She sorted through the bookcase and removed *Hoot Owl, Little Women* and *Huckleberry Finn*, books she had bought with her own money; then she thought better of it and put them back for next year's pupils. Miss Self had taught her last year.

In the bottom drawer of her desk, pushed to the back, she came across a large brown envelope; she hadn't seen the contents for many years. Carefully she took out the yellowed paper dated April 12, 1922: *"When I Become a Schoolteacher by Chastity Giberson. Besides teaching arithmetic and history, I will make sure my pupils read good books, and maybe some day they will be inspired to write even better books of their own —"*

Miss Self finished reading the short English theme, a single page written in a neat hand. Her eyes filled with tears at the inequity of life. She wrote a note to Cappy asking him to stop by.

The day after Cappy received the note, he drove directly from work to White School, borrowing the family car that day. He hadn't been to his old school since eighth-grade graduation, and had seen Miss Self only in passing.

The sight of his old school caused a sudden, unexpected longing. He remembered his first day, with Worthy dragging him by the collar, and the grief he had caused Miss Self for eight years. And Beany Ozbun, the new boy who couldn't do anything a boy his age was supposed to do.

Everything in sight needed paint — the schoolhouse, the coal shed — and the outhouses were in shambles, turned over too many Halloweens. He stepped onto the porch; the boards were so rotted he could see the ground underneath.

"Cap, come in." Miss Self smiled when she saw the handsome young man. "I'd know you anywhere, the image of Chastity."

Cappy was taken aback by the direct reference to his mother.

Miss Self handed him the paper. "This is something your mother wrote, three years before her death, three years before you were born. She was a brilliant girl, but I suppose you've heard all this many times."

"No, I haven't." Neither Willa nor Worthy had been forthcoming when he asked questions about his mother, and so he'd finally stopped asking.

"Then it's time you heard. Your mother had a special gift. From the first day, I thought she would go far."

"But she quit school early, the same as Tick," Cappy said.

"You're right. Her quitting after seventh grade was all Worthy's doing." Thinking about their long-ago confrontation still made her pulse quicken. "But in fairness to the man, he believed he was doing right."

"But he didn't make me quit —"

"To Worthy's way of thinking, school was for boys if they were so inclined, but girls, especially pretty girls like Chastity, should prepare themselves for marriage. No matter what I said, he wouldn't budge from his decision."

"Tell me more about what she was like — my mother."

"In all my years of teaching, she was leagues above any student I've ever had. I thought you had some of her ability, but you had so much devilment. . . . She was good in every subject, but English was her forte. At eleven, she could write a better story than most adults."

Several quiet minutes passed, Miss Self lost in some far-away time, Cappy in his own memories. Finally, Cappy folded the composition and put it in his pocket.

"There's one other thing," she said, reaching back into the envelope. "A picture of my 1922 class, the only picture I ever took of students. It's also yours to keep."

Cappy held the old photograph gingerly, scanning the smiling faces for one he might recognize.

He found his mother standing in the front row — her plaid dress short, her long cotton stockings falling down around her knees. A March wind was gusting that day, and her blond hair was blowing away from her face. She looked happy.

"Thank you, Miss Self," he said, awkwardly shaking her thin, cold hand.

Two weeks after the end of the school year, Margaret Self died — her virginity and her cancer intact. Cappy wrote an obituary even finer than Willie Biesemeyer's.

Chapter XVII

As Cappy did every morning when he first arrived at work, he knocked on Asbury's door for his day's assignments. He was surprised to hear Min Wollums's voice telling him to come in. She was sitting at Asbury's desk, typing, in a dress that resembled a polka-dotted tent.

"What's on your mind?" she asked, not looking up.

"I'm here to see the boss." Cappy was conscious he was thinking like Worthy.

"Az is off slaying dragons, so I'm the boss now. From today on, running the paper is up to me."

Cappy didn't know what she meant about slaying dragons, but he guessed it had something to do with the war.

"You're still unseasoned, Cappy," Min said, finally interrupting her typing, "but you've got imagination. Poor Az doesn't have enough imagination to write his own obituary. This is my newspaper, I bought and paid for it, and now I'm going to run it."

Cappy stared at the huge woman, suddenly angry at Asbury for leaving him at his wife's mercy.

She smiled as if she could read his thoughts. "Here's how it is, Cappy. What I lack in experience, I'll make up in savvy. You've heard of playing music by ear? Well, that's my approach to running this paper."

"I've got some ideas for editorials to write —"

"I'll be writing the editorials."

"I never heard of a woman running a newspaper," Cappy grumbled. Now, he *knew* he was thinking like Worthy.

"There aren't many women editors, but I'm prepared to work however long it takes to make this paper one of the best in the state. I'll expect you and everyone on the payroll to be available day or night, even Sundays occasionally, to help me get the job done. Are you agreeable?"

"All but Sundays. That's my time for helping at home."

"You can have your Sundays, but keep yourself free the other six days. Evenings included."

Before Cappy could protest, Min went back to her typing.

AFTER WORK, CAPPY WENT HOME and found a letter from Beany; he read it to Willa and Worthy during supper.

Dear Farm Boy,

This is my last letter for a while. We're being sent overseas, but don't worry. I've never heard of anybody in Special Services being a target (unless the music stinks!). Even though I won't be in the fighting I still can't write to you. The worst part of Army life is being told what to do and when to do it, and not being able to play Chopin. Everybody wants to hear popular tunes, so that's what we have to give them. But playing the piano sure beats pointing a gun at somebody. See you when the war's over or I go A.W.O.L., whichever comes first!

Your pal,
Beany.

Cappy read the letter again, alone this time, and put it in a box under his bed. If only he could be allowed to enlist. After reading a few pages of *This Side of Paradise,* a book he loved, with light practiced stroking, he lulled himself to sleep.

Chapter XVIII

~

*W*hile all of Old Kane's citizens sacrificed and pulled together to help the war effort — making bandages from old undergarments, collecting scrap metal to be melted and reshaped into tanks — Cappy was most proud of Willa. By 1943, she had been spotting airplanes for the United States government for more than a year. She had been provided a pamphlet showing silhouettes of Allied and enemy planes, and her job was to identify and count each plane that went overhead, noting in particular the time and direction.

Each morning when her kitchen work was finished, she took a pair of binoculars and climbed to a clearing atop MacElroy Hill. As she was not supposed to leave her post unless she had something to report, she took along a bread-and-butter sandwich and a red delicious apple for lunch. She told Worthy it was his patriotic duty to fend for himself at noontime for the duration of the war. Cappy imagined

Willa, farm-bound for sixty-seven years, examining the skies in wonder.

On a Friday evening in August, Worthy came in late from the fields expecting to smell supper cooking, but the only scent in the dark kitchen was from a fresh bouquet of wildflowers on the sideboard. Sensing things were not in order, he grabbed a lantern and went looking for Willa.

By the time he reached the bottom of MacElroy Hill the sky was black, no moon or stars to ease the night. He began the steep climb, stopping now and then to get his breath. When he was nearly at the top of the hill he tripped over a prone figure. Expecting the worst, he leaned down and put his ear to Willa's chest. She was breathing, shallowly, and her eyes were open. He called her name, trying to get her to answer, but she was unable to speak. Swearing softly, he picked her up and carried her down the hill and into the house. With great care, he stretched her out on the front room davenport and placed a cushion under her head.

Within twenty minutes, Doc Potter was listening to Willa's heart and taking her blood pressure. Worthy paced back and forth between the front room and the kitchen. He had not felt so helpless since he had watched Chastity die.

"She doesn't look good," Doc Potter said. He shone a light into her blank eyes. "How old is Willa?"

"Sixty-seven her last birthday," Worthy said. "She sure as hell ain't old enough to die on me. I've always been the frail one." Doc Potter gave a muted laugh.

"One thing being a doctor has taught me, Worthy, there's no rhyme or reason to life and death."

Worthy stopped pacing. "What are you saying, Doc?"

"She's had a stroke. Leave her here on the davenport for the night, make sure she stays warm, and I'll be back first thing tomorrow for another look. That's all we can do for now. Willa's going to need a lot of caring for, and all that pacing around won't help her."

"Should I fix her something to eat? I ain't exactly handy with the stove."

"Maybe tomorrow you can try giving her a little oatmeal, but for now the most you can do is hold her hand and let her know you're here with her."

"I'll do that, all right. I'll pull a chair up and stay in plain sight so she won't be scared."

"I'll see you first thing in the morning. And don't worry about Cappy. Young people handle these bumps in the road better than us old codgers."

Worthy watched as the old doctor shuffled out to his car and, from sheer determination and years of practice, heaved himself into the driver's seat. He sat by Willa's side all night watching for any sign of movement, and sometimes speaking her name so she would know he was there. He thought how just the evening before they had sat by the radio laughing at the *Judy Canova Show*.

By the time the doctor returned the next morning, Willa's eyes were as wide open as Mary Lee Margeson's dime-store baby. She could neither move nor speak.

"Looks like a bad one," Doc Potter said. "See this?" He pinched Willa's arm. "She doesn't feel a thing. At least if she does, the message isn't getting to her brain.

"Think about getting help for Willa," Doc said as he

repacked his black bag. "I'll be surprised if she ever gets off that davenport under her own power."

Doc had barely gone when Cappy arrived; he had worked late and slept on the couch at the office. "What was Doc doing here?" he called from the kitchen, as he poured a glass of milk. "I met him as I was rounding Prough's Corner."

Worthy didn't answer right away, trying to think what to say.

"Cap, there's no easy way to tell you this —" He stopped to get control of his voice. "It's your ma. She was on MacElroy Hill and had a stroke. She can't talk or move."

Cappy set his glass down and walked into the front room. He stood quietly and looked at the still figure that barely resembled Willa — her eyes vacant, her mouth slack. "Maybe I'll fix us some breakfast," he said finally, the only words he could trust himself to speak.

Cappy cracked a dozen brown eggs into a crock, as he had seen Willa do over the years. He mixed in some top cream, a little salt and pepper, and dropped the mixture into a cast-iron skillet. While the eggs cooked, he cut up an onion and a piece of longhorn cheese and added them to the bubbling eggs. He sliced a loaf of soda bread that Willa had baked fresh that morning before leaving for MacElroy Hill. He carried a plate of the hot food to Worthy, who let it grow cold.

Cappy sat alone at the kitchen table staring at his food. He couldn't imagine not seeing Willa bustling around the house, fixing meals, counting eggs and airplanes. Memories of her came back in a rush: her pride when he graduated from high school; the look of wonder when Ned Helvy walked onto the stage; her sadness when Tick left.

OLD KANE WOMAN CASUALTY OF WAR

Willa Giberson, wife of Worthy Giberson, has become a casualty while serving her country. She was highly valued for her skill at counting, and helped the war effort by keeping an exact tally of planes that flew over Greene County. As she is no longer able to continue her valuable work, it's the duty of all Old Kane citizens to watch the skies on her behalf.

"WHAT WAS YOU THINKING ABOUT, writing that goddamned article?" Worthy shouted at Cappy. "I ain't had a minute's peace since the paper come out, and tell me if you will, what in the name of Jesus am I to do with all them sweet stuffs everybody brought. Willa ain't dead yet!"

"I never said one word that wasn't the truth!" Cappy stormed out of the house and slammed the door behind him. It was obvious that he and Worthy could not discuss the real source of their anger. Worthy had taught him well; a man's feelings are meant to be held in.

Later, Cappy peeked into the front room. Worthy was sitting close to Willa, the two of them listening to the *Grand Ole Opry* as if it were an ordinary Saturday Night. Cappy tiptoed up the stairs to his room and started a letter to Beany.

Dear Beany,

I need somebody to talk to tonight and it looks like you're it. Ma had a bad stroke and it looks like she won't get well. I feel sorry for her, but I'm sorriest for myself. I wouldn't say that to anybody but you. Maybe it's guilty I'm feeling. I keep remembering times Ma wanted to talk about when she was growing up, or what her folks were like, her own Ma especially, and I didn't want to listen. And now it's too late and I'll never hear those stories. Did you know she traveled from Kentucky to Illinois in a covered wagon when she was a little girl? I wish the war was over.

Cappy.

Chapter XIX

*W*ithin a month of Willa's stroke, Billy Dupré walked up the lane to the house where he had grown up. He was nattily dressed in a white shirt and tie and new suit pants; over one arm he carried a new suit coat that matched the pants. His teeth were as even and white as a movie star's; they, too, were new. His hair was as platinum as Min Wollums's and his cheeks suggested a touch of rouge. Five years earlier Tick Giberson had left Old Kane, but it was Billy Dupré returning. He knocked on the screen door, nervous as when he preached his first sermon.

Worthy did not recognize him. "What can I do for you, stranger?"

"Pa, it's me, your second-born."

It took a minute for Worthy to understand. "Tick!" Awkwardly he hugged his long-lost son. "But what in God's name happened to your looks? I near mistook you for a moving picture actor!"

Tick blushed at what he took to be a compliment. "Thanks, Pa. My looks is not all that's changed. I even got me a new name, Billy Dupré. Reverend Art picked it out."

"So it's 'Billy Dupré' now. Christ, you even *sound* like a movie actor. You're just what the doctor ordered!" Worthy said, shaking Tick's soft, manicured hand. "If I believed in prayer, you'd be the walking answer."

"Ma's the reason I'm here. I come across a copy of the Carrollton paper in my travels, and saw Cappy's item about her being sick."

"Well, I'm proud you're here. We'll go to the front room, that's where she's at, and you can see what you think. We'll have ourselves a bite to eat and afterwards you can commence the healing. But first take a look at her to get an idea what you're up against." Again, Worthy wondered about the power of prayer. If anyone could heal Willa, it would be her own son.

Worthy led the way into the front room where Willa had been lying since the stroke. Tick looked down at his mother. "She's awake," he said, "her eyes are wide open."

"That don't mean nothing, they're always open. Now about this healing. Where do we start?"

"Pa, I hate letting you down, but I can't heal without Reverend Art standing next to me. It's him who figures out who can be healed. Say we're in a meeting and an old lady hobbles up front with a lame leg, not one that's broke but merely lame — I speak in tongues and she'll walk back to her seat good as new. But if a mother comes up front carrying a blind baby, Reverend Art tells the crowd that blind babies is the will of God and we're not meant to butt in."

"Maybe we could take Willa to the church. That's where healing is most likely to take place."

"But Pa, you ain't hearing what I say. If there's any healing, it's because the sick person's brain helps out. And it's plain to see Ma's brain ain't in no shape to help."

"Then why in the name of Jesus did you come and raise my hopes?" For the first time in his life, Worthy's face betrayed his deep despair.

"I come to pay my respects."

"If you can't heal, how about if you stay and help out around the farm? I've got Shag Kallal feeding and milking, but he ain't up to handling fence mending or figuring a cow's time to breed. If it wasn't for the neighbors helping out, my crops would be rotting in the fields. My days are took up in the house cooking mush or oatmeal and trying to get Willa to swallow. Christ, some days the food falls out of her mouth faster than I can poke it back in. I have to keep a bib on her like she's a baby. And the washing, I never seen so much!" Worthy realized that until now, he had not spoken his feelings.

Tick looked at his gold watch. "It's getting late, Pa. We're having a big tent meeting over in Hardin tonight, and I need to be on the noon bus. Give my regards to Ma if she ever wakes up."

"Ain't you gonna wait around to see Cappy?"

"Not this time, Pa, but I'll be back. Tell Cappy I've learned a lot of new things to teach him first chance I get."

Worthy watched as Tick walked down the lane, becoming Billy Dupré again with every step.

THE BUS WAS BARELY UNDERWAY to Hardin when it ran off the road. Billy Dupré stood at the front of the tipped bus and gave a blessing in tongues. Passengers went away claiming they were spared because God had put Billy Dupré on the noon bus.

When Min Wollums heard of the accident, she called Cappy into her office. "I want you to talk to the passengers," she said, "and be sure to check out a preacher named Billy Dupré who was on the bus. The passengers are giving him credit for saving their lives, divine intervention they're calling it. He's preaching in a tent in Hardin the rest of the week. Be there tonight and see what he's got to say."

AT SEVEN O'CLOCK THE ORGANIST PLAYED A FANFARE and two identically dressed men strutted down the center aisle of the Hardin tent to the platform. They had matching platinum hair and carried matching white Bibles.

Cappy was sitting in the front row. He recognized the older man as Reverend Art Gimmy. He did not recognize the younger man, but assumed he was Billy Dupré.

Prior to passing the collection plates, Reverend Art told the dramatic story of the bus accident. "Tonight the passengers on that bus are thanking Billy Dupré for saving their lives," Reverend Art said, "and those of you here tonight should dig deep into your pockets so Billy can keep up his good works." The plates came back overflowing with paper money.

After several stirring revival choruses, Billy Dupré himself was introduced. To music only he could hear, he swayed from side to side, like a hootchy-kootchy dancer at the county fair. The congregation followed his lead, slowly waving their arms and moaning low.

Then, as if from a cue offstage, Billy stopped dancing and stood perfectly still. Not a sound came from the audience; even the children were strangely quiet. Billy opened his mouth and began to speak rapidly, his eyes closed, his eyelids fluttering, in a language Cappy could not place. After twenty minutes, Billy said "Amen", and left the tent.

Cappy approached the sweaty evangelist and held out his hand. "My name's Cappy Giberson, and I work for the *Democrat-Republican Patriot*. I'm here to inquire about the bus wreck this morning."

"I was on it, all right," Billy said. Cappy looked exactly like Chastity.

"Would you say the wreck was the driver's fault?"

"I'd say it was mostly the Devil's fault, with a little help from the driver." Billy ran a comb through his glowing hair. Then he laughed gleefully.

"What?" Cappy took a step forward.

Billy laughed again at the look on Cappy's face. "You don't know me from Adam!"

Cappy looked closer. "Tick?" He couldn't help himself; he threw his arms around his brother. "What happened to your hair — and your name?

"Changing them was Reverend Art's idea. I'd still rather go by Tick but I'm getting used to Billy. And the hair suits me. Girls are partial to light hair; you ought to know that. Have I got some lessons to teach you!"

Cappy punched Tick affectionately. "I hate to bring bad news, but a few weeks ago Ma had a stroke."

179

"I know, I was by the house this morning. Pa was in a sweat because I couldn't heal her. It looks to me like her soul's already in heaven and her body don't know it."

"Are you saying you buy all that shit Reverend Art pushes, about heaven and healing?" Cappy was aware he might be probing too far, too early.

"Reverend Art himself don't believe it in total, but telling the story puts bread and wine on the table. Them's his words. Take a look at my watch, it's real gold. And I've got me a car but I can't drive it yet." The old Tick was becoming more apparent.

"This revival business — doesn't it bother you the way you're bilking money in return for fakery?" Cappy was surprised at the harshness of his question.

"We ain't bilking money. We just tell folks how good they'll feel after emptying their pockets for the Lord, and it works every time. What's the harm in a little storytelling if folks is made happy. Ain't that what Pa preaches? Cappy, I've got feelings about Ma the same as you, but I work for God, the way you work for that paper. I don't see you giving *that* up to stay home with Ma."

"I'll try to do better if you will." The brothers shook hands and Tick walked back into the tent. Soon Billy Dupré was on stage again.

Cappy was left to sort out the evening's happenings. This is one story Min Wollums will never get to edit, he thought, as he wondered what excuse he would give her.

Chapter XX

After Willa's stroke, on Friday nights without fail Bum showed up to keep Worthy company. On one such night in December, as he limped up the lane, he noticed that every light in the house was off, even the one in the front room. Letting himself in, he found Worthy sitting in the dark.

"I didn't see no need of wasting juice lighting up the place," Worthy commented. "Willa don't know light from dark, and by now I know every inch of this room by heart. Maybe I'm helping win the war by not using so many lights. What the hell difference does it make?"

Bum understood that his old friend was feeling sorry for himself.

"There's something I been meaning to bring up, Worthy. A thief could of walked in that front door as easy as me and stole everything in sight. Myself, I never set foot out of the house without first making sure the door's latched. You'd do well to follow suit."

Worthy ignored his friend's advice. "What's in the sack?" he asked. Bum never called without bringing a bag of peanuts or a cream soda.

"Something new." Bum dumped the contents onto the lamp table. "Devil's food cupcakes with white filling inside every cake. It's a puzzle to me how they get that filling to stay on the inside. You'd think it would run out all over the oven."

He looked down at Willa, a gesture to show interest in his friend's burden. "She gets more shrunken every time I see her. At least when my Imadean passed, she was plump and pretty near healthy. I'm thankful I didn't have to look at her in such a shape as your Willa."

"You know, she's the only woman I ever laid with," Worthy said unexpectedly. "I'll never forget our wedding night and her hiding under the covers, gritting her teeth against me —"

Bum began to fidget. Although he and Worthy had been friends since boyhood, there were some topics not proper to be discussed, especially in the company of the party in question.

"I figured it was natural for a female to grit her teeth the first coupling with a male," Worthy went on, "but I fully expected in time she'd get used to it. Jesus, Bum, if only once in all them years Willa had give in without gritting her teeth! But I don't fault her. It was that goddamned mother of hers — and her Baptist teachings. Even after the woman passed on she still had a hold over Willa."

"Some men would of looked elsewhere," Bum said.

"There's the rub. In spite of all her holding back and her narrow ways, she was the only woman I wanted."

Bum had never seen Worthy so low.

He immediately brought up about how it hadn't rained in a month, and how the war seemed to be going in favor of the Allies. As the mantel clock struck ten, Bum stood up to leave. "Well, time I was heading out. I'll be back next Friday night. Leave a light burning so I don't trip and break my good leg."

THE FOLLOWING NIGHT, the Woosley Twins paid a visit to the Giberson farm. The twins stood outside the house for an hour watching through the dimly-lit front-room window.

"Jesus, my balls is about froze off," George said, shivering. "If Worthy don't go to bed soon I'm for leaving."

At eight o'clock they could vaguely make out Worthy preparing for his nightly trip to the outhouse. He took along a lantern and a copy of *Country Gentleman,* a clear indication he planned to be a while.

Ralph was first through the door, George close behind. "Let's try the upstairs first," Ralph said. "I plan on going away from here a few dollars richer."

They split up to search the bedrooms. George lingered in what had been Chastity's room, her gingham dresses still hanging in the closet, pressed and ready to wear. He lifted the skirt of a pink dress and held it to his nose, but the years had claimed the girl-scent he hoped to find. A small wood box on top of her bureau held a row of Sunday School pins for seven years' perfect attendance. He left the pins where they were, sticking by his vow never to steal anything of a religious nature.

Ralph searched the boys' bedrooms to no avail. (He glanced through the box under Cappy's bed, but it was full of papers.) He was going through the dresser drawers in Worthy and Willa's bedroom when George joined him. Together they looked through the rest of the drawers and the closet, and got down on the floor with a flashlight to look under the bed. Then, they put everything back carefully.

"Shit, what a waste of time," Ralph said, "Drayton will laugh when we come away empty-handed."

They went back through the house the way they had come, passing through the front room again. This time they stopped to look at Willa.

"Christ, she's spooky as hell," George said. He stared down at the rigid woman, her wide eyes accusing him. "I've heard it said Worthy won't leave her side except to take a crap like he's doing now."

On his way out the front door, George grabbed a small celluloid Kewpie doll from the hallway table.

When Worthy stepped inside his kitchen, he stopped short. Something ain't right, he thought. I can smell it. He searched upstairs and down, but could not find anything disturbed. He thought briefly of Bum's warnings about locking his door, before noticing that Willa's favorite Kewpie doll was missing from the hall.

ANY TIME THE WOOSLEY TWINS were on their own, Drayton Hunt was concerned. It was hard to tell what they might do out from under his watchful eye. But he had sent them to ransack Worthy's house, and when they reported back they had found nothing of value, Drayton exploded in anger.

But I'll get what I want one of these days, he thought. More important to Worthy and me than any money. My son.

Chapter XXI

By January 7, 1944, General Dwight D. Eisenhower was in London, amassing men, ships and guns for the invasion of Europe. D-Day would come on June 6. Cappy was busier than ever at the paper. Daily he was approached by this one and that one around Old Kane, each with an anecdote (usually about themselves) they believed would make interesting reading. Where business owners, farmers, and housewives were once closemouthed, they now saw it as an honor if Cappy Giberson wrote about them. It was understood, and expected, that he would add a bit here and there in the tradition of good storytelling.

One such person agitating to be interviewed was Drayton Hunt; an idea had been gnawing away at him for months. Finally he stopped by the newspaper office and told Min Wollums what he wanted. After he left, she called Cappy into her office.

"No, I won't do it," Cappy said angrily. "Drayton Hunt is

no better than a bully, and on top of that, he eggs on the Woosley Twins. Pa despises him."

"Repugnant as the idea sounds, you'll learn something from the experience," Min replied. "And a reporter can't be selective based on personal feelings." She smiled and ruffled his hair. "I told the Hunt fellow you'd be at his house this afternoon at two o'clock."

Min was the boss. Cappy would follow her orders but he would not have to like them.

After a hamburger sandwich at Day's Café, Cappy drove the old family Chevy to Mae Hunt's place. Drayton, at forty-three, still lived with his mother. Cappy took a deep breath and knocked on the front door.

"Do come in, Mr. Cappy," Drayton said, his voice strangely soft. He was amused that Cappy mirrored his own tall, thin frame. Drayton was wearing a dark-colored shirt and good trousers and puffing on a strong, sweet cigar. A thin black mustache decorated his crooked upper lip, and a missing front tooth had been replaced with a silver replica.

"Well, now," Drayton said, "you and me has not come in direct contact with one another since you was a tyke. I recall offering you a dime once, but Worthy wouldn't let you have it. Worthy always did have it in for me."

Cappy did not remember the incident.

Cappy sat in a soft overstuffed chair, its arms covered with white lace doilies. In one corner stood a large floor radio. The station was playing a Freddie Slack record; the big bass speaker made Cappy feel like he was hearing Freddie in person. In another corner a mahogany curio was filled with figurines of little girls in long dresses, and a polished lectern held a leather-bound family Bible. Warm air from two registers in the floor took away the January chill. The room was not what Cappy had expected.

Drayton returned carrying coffee and a small plate piled high with sweets. The perfect host, Cappy thought grudgingly, as he bit into a cherry tart.

But immediately Drayton said something offensive. "Say, didn't your poor mama pass on when you was born? No need to feel ashamed of not knowing your pa. I don't know who mine was, either. Looks like you and me has got a lot in common!" Drayton had thought to tell Cappy the truth about their relationship, but at that moment decided he would wait until the telling would gain him the most.

Cappy's stomach was roiling at the notion that he and Drayton Hunt had anything in common. "Min Wollums says you have a story for the paper. You can start talking and I'll write it down."

"I like a man who gets right to business, something else you and me has got in common. Well, it's like this. I was driving my Moon down Main Street one day noticing the motorcars parked in front of businesses, mostly Fords and Chevies, and it come to me that I'm driving the only car of its kind around Old Kane. They quit making Moons in 1929, you know. That's what I want you to write about — how Drayton R. Hunt of Old Kane, Illinois, drives a 1924 Moon sedan, and how it looks and runs like a brand new motorcar."

"That sounds interesting enough," Cappy said, relieved. "You can start by giving me the name of the company that made it, the horsepower, how many miles it's gone —"

"The Moon Motor Car Company out of St. Louis built it," Drayton swelled with pride. "'Priced Within the Bounds of Reason' was the slogan they used, but that don't mean it was cheap. It was modeled after a Rolls Royce. How about if I was to take you for a spin? You can set in the front seat and write down how you feel riding in it and what the country-side looks like whizzing by. The way I see it, it's better to screw some sweet young thing yourself than have your best buddy report on what it's like."

Drayton's analogy went over Cappy's head, but since he was a boy, he had been curious about the fancy motorcar. "All right, I'll go for a ride, a short one."

Cappy settled into the soft, royal blue cushions on the passenger's side while Drayton cranked the engine. He wrote in his notebook that the car did not have even one scratch on its finish, and the engine hummed like it was fresh from the factory.

"I'll keep quiet so you can pay strict attention to your feelings," Drayton said. He watched Cappy as he turned onto the gravel road.

In spite of himself, Cappy enjoyed the ride; the car took the corners as smoothly as Min Wollums's 1940 Lincoln Zephyr. Drayton drove for several miles, then turned onto a narrow dirt road that wound around through the frozen countryside. They went up and over Wisdom Hill, and crossed the Macoupin Creek Bridge into Coal Hollow.

"Shit! It just come to me!" Drayton said, interrupting Cappy's appreciation. "I've took this same route before! And guess who was setting in the very seat you're setting in. Your own sweet mama! Ain't it a small world?"

Cappy focused his eyes on the passing hills and valleys.

"Yes, sir, your mama was something special, all right, with that long silky yellow hair of hers, and you should of seen her titties, not too big, not too little." He let the car coast to a stop and turned off the motor. "And here's the very spot I stopped so she could admire the wildflowers. Your mama was always pestering me to drive her out in the country to look at the flowers. Of course I knew what she had on her mind, and it sure as hell wasn't wildflowers."

Cappy stared at Drayton in horror. "You don't know anything about my mother!"

"Take it easy, boy. I was merely acting the gentleman by screwing your mama. Hell, I may even be your daddy!" This was the first time Drayton had spoken those words to anyone but Worthy. They felt good on his tongue.

"You son of a bitch!" Cappy landed a blow that bloodied Drayton's nose, got out of the Moon and started running across the fields in a sudden freezing rain.

Drayton watched Cappy make his way across the barren field. "Like mama, like son!" he laughed, as he dabbed at his swelling nose. He put the Moon in gear and drove home, savoring what was to come.

BY THE TIME CAPPY KNOCKED ON MIN'S DOOR, his anger had not subsided, but as he inhaled the aroma of chili spices, he was reminded of how he missed walking into his own house and smelling Willa's supper frying on the stove. He could not remember the last time he had been this hungry.

Min led him into her living room where places were set on the coffee table. Since Asbury had left for some secret job in the OSS, she had lost 50 pounds on a diet of cottage cheese and grapefruit. Now the only sound she made as she walked across the room was a gentle swish. As soon as Cappy was settled on the sofa, she carried in a tray with two large bowls of hot chili, and dishes of saltines and dill pickles.

While they ate, Cappy told her of his encounter with Drayton Hunt. She nodded in understanding, sometimes touching his hand. "Next time I'll listen when you have objections," she said. "Now let's talk of something else. How's your mother? Any improvement?"

"No. I'm used to her condition, but I can't get used to Pa's. He'll spend an hour getting a little oatmeal or soup down her throat. He even eats the stuff himself. He says he can't choke down pork chops and potatoes while she has to eat like a baby. They're both thin as rails."

As they talked, Min moved closer to Cappy; he noticed how nice she smelled. He leaned his head against her shoulder and immediately fell asleep. He jumped awake as the hall clock struck ten. "Sorry I went to sleep. I was worn out."

"Why not stay the night? I could use some company."

"I guess I can do that. Pa won't notice if I'm home or not."

She led the way upstairs to a large bedroom; blue flowered wallpaper, blue bedspread, blue frilly curtains. "You can warm the bed for me," she said. "I'll just be a minute." She closed the bathroom door behind her. He could hear the faucet running.

Cappy was surprised at not having his own room, the house as large as it was, but Min seemed lonesome for company. He took off his clothes and quickly got under the heavy blankets.

Min came back wearing a silky, blue nightgown. "I've been missing a man in my bed," she said, snuggling close. "I suppose you've had lots of girls, a good-looking boy like you?"

"I had a girl once, Dimple Boston, but I never *had* her, if that's what you're getting at. She was afraid I'd mess her hairdo."

"Well, this girl isn't afraid of having her hairdo messed." Min slipped the nightgown from her shoulders and allowed Cappy to see her breasts. He thought they were beautiful — smooth and white. It occurred to him he had never seen Dimple's.

At Min's urging, Cappy lay back on the bed and she took the lead. She let the nightgown slip the rest of the way down her body, then bent over and kissed his mouth. She tasted of citrus.

With deliberation, she began to caress here, lick there. Starting at Cappy's nipples, she moved down his body with her tongue. She licked his inner thighs, delighting in his quick response. When he thought he would burst from excitement, she guided him into her. From that point, Cappy knew what to do as if he had been doing it all his life — just as Worthy once predicted.

Before starting work next morning, Cappy walked into Min's office without knocking. He stood in front of her desk waiting to be acknowledged.

"Do you want something?" she asked, barely glancing up from her typewriter.

"I sure had a good time last night." He was about to leap over the desk and kiss her when she looked up. "Cappy, before you start getting the wrong idea, nothing has changed between you and me. I'm your boss and you're a young man learning to write. Last night we had some fun, nothing more. Don't start thinking of me as your 'girl' and don't tell your friends. Now I have a lot of work to do, and I'm sure you do, too."

Crushed, but needing to tell somebody everything, Cappy started a letter to Beany, wherever he might be.

You're reading a letter from someone who now knows a woman in the Biblical sense, if you catch my meaning. Last night I went to my boss's house and slept in her bed. With her! It was every bit as good as I've heard. My folks would have a fit, but married women already know what to do and that's a definite advantage. You might want to keep that in mind. I'll be glad when you get home safe from wherever you are. Your adulterous friend, Cappy.

Chapter XXII

On the third Thursday of every January, the Old Kane High School gymnasium was the site of the March of Dimes Dance. Receipts went to fight infantile paralysis, a disease that crippled children and adults. President Roosevelt, a victim himself, claimed even the poorest family could spare a dime.

For as long as anyone could remember, Worthy had been in charge of hiring the band, primarily because he was judged to be the best square dancer in Greene County, at the same time capable of handling the foxtrot. But because of Willa's condition, the job of hiring the band in 1944 fell to Cappy.

"There ain't many bands that still carries a fiddler," Worthy told Cappy. "And don't forget your caller. Kilby Cotter's the best if you catch him when his gums ain't sore. Once he takes his teeth out, you can't understand a word he says. And you're looking at two dollars for Kilby alone. You'll have to draw a big crowd if there's to be any money left over for the cripples. One other thing, see to it the floor gets sprinkled with dance wax. Square dancers ain't happy if their feet don't slip and slide all over the place."

"I'll do the best I can," Cappy said, "but it's not easy filling your shoes, Pa."

THE WOOSLEY TWINS AND DRAYTON HUNT were also discussing the dance. "It's the one night of the year every house in Greene County will be empty as my pockets," Ralph said. "We can make a cleaning!"

"Ralph's right," George said. "While everybody's in town dancing the box-step, we can be waltzing from one house to the next without any barrier whatsoever."

"You poor dumb bastards!" Drayton said. "If everybody's at the gymnasium except us three, who do you think winds up catching the blame if something's missing?"

"There wouldn't be no proof," Ralph said.

"Forget it," Drayton said. "I'm going to the dance and help buy an iron lung for some sick baby."

THE NIGHT OF THE DANCE, a foot of new snow lay on the ground, but it would take more than a snowstorm to keep Old Kane at home. There were few enough pleasures in wartime.

The women and girls wore flaring, full skirts and the scents of "Evening in Paris" and "Blue Waltz" perfumes hung heavily in the air. The men and boys dressed as if they were on their way to church, with ties and jackets. Drayton Hunt showed up in a zoot suit with padded shoulders and high-waisted trousers. All the men had skipped their morning shaves in favor of an evening date with the razor.

The Amona Class of the Baptist Church, given special dispensation by Brother Beams to attend if they promised not to engage in any dancing, set a table with fruit punch and date cookies. Shirley Jean Goode, the previous summer's infantile paralysis victim, was wheeled in as a reminder of the disease being celebrated. Her wheelchair was placed beneath the south basketball hoop where she could watch the festivities.

The band opened with "Don't Fence Me In", a lively new song, and the floor quickly filled up, couples happily bumping into each other as they danced a combination two-step and jitterbug.

The woman eliciting the most attention was Min Wollums. In the interest of promoting goodwill for the newspaper, Min had driven down from Carrollton to attend. Her platinum hair and full figure drew glances from every direction. When Cappy danced with Min, she drew him so close a wheat straw couldn't pass between them. He was embarrassed; stories were circulating throughout Old Kane, but Min *was* his boss.

The band played "Little White Lies" and "It's Only a Paper Moon", hits from a dozen years back, before Kirby Cotter yelled, "Fill up the floor for a square!"

Anyone under twenty was expected to sit out the squares, an unspoken rule. Nothing upset the old-timers quicker than having a teenage boy or girl circling the wrong direction in "Eight Hands 'Round".

Drayton bided his time. When the break ended, he swaggered toward Min, puffing on a cigarette.

"Why, hello there, pretty lady. How about a dance?" He grinned at Min as if he knew her well.

Min resigned herself to dancing with the devil. Drayton knew all the steps but he lacked any semblance of rhythm. He dipped and twirled Min without matching his feet to the drumbeat.

When the band eased the dancers into a ballad, Drayton tried again. "How about taking another turn with me?" he said to Min.

"No, thank you. I've promised every dance."

Cappy walked up. "I'm here for our dance, Min." He took his boss in his arms and foxtrotted off to "I'll See You In My Dreams". Spurned, Drayton withdrew in anger. He felt like a fool in front of the crowd.

Drayton spotted a young man in uniform enter the gymnasium. The soldier stood for a minute looking around the crowd, then walked among the dancers and tapped Cappy on the shoulder.

"Out of my way, kid," he said, reaching for Min Wollums's hand. "I've come all the way from Europe for a dance with this lady."

"Beany!" Cappy was dumbstruck. "How come you didn't let me know you were coming?"

"I wanted to see the surprised look on your face — and it was worth it!"

"Are you on leave? How long have you got?" Cappy had a dozen more questions.

"Later. I can see you've got other things on your mind." He smiled at Min.

Drayton watched the scene with growing anger. He knew how chummy Cappy and the Ozbun boy had been over the years, and it rankled him. There was something about Beany Ozbun that got under his skin, but he couldn't put a name to it.

Cappy and Beany stayed until the band was packed up and the last person had left, making sure the lights were turned off and the doors locked. They walked out together, catching up on happenings since they had last seen each other. Beany talked of Army life, and how the war seemed to be winding down, and how glad he was to be on furlough, even if it was short. Beany got into Cappy's car and they continued talking; the windows fogged from their warm breath.

"What will you be doing when you go back?" Cappy asked.

"We'll be working up a new show and they'll send us somewhere to put it on for the troops. If I had to be in the Army, I can't think of a better outfit to be in. All the guys are great. But I'm sure tired of playing nothing but popular music. That'll change when I get into college."

"I made a deal with Asbury that I'd go to college when the war's over," Cappy said, "so it looks like we're headed in the same direction."

They talked until their cars were covered again with a light dusting of new snow. Finally Cappy said, "I'd better be going, Min's expecting me. See you tomorrow." His wheels spun as he started up, spraying Beany with snow. "Sorry Old

Bean!" Cappy yelled out the window. "Say, you look better covered with snow!" he laughed.

"You'll be sorry!" Beany yelled back. He made a ball of wet snow and hurled it through the open window. It struck Cappy full in the face. "Now who's laughing!" He stood and watched, smiling at his friend, until Cappy's car was out of sight.

Beany was tired and eager to get home, but when he put the car in gear, the engine choked a couple of times and died. He tried again to restart it, grinding the starter until there was no more sound, but the engine wouldn't turn over. With a feeling of helplessness, he got out and tried to raise the hood, not that he would know what to do when he got it open, but it was frozen shut. Looks like I'll be walking home, he thought. At least the snow had stopped.

Chapter XXIII

Worthy had gone to bed before dark, but sleep eluded him. He tried picturing the crowd at the dance, counting couples instead of sheep, but his eyes stayed open as wide as Willa's.

For the past week Willa had not once closed her eyes, not even to blink. Her pupils continued to dilate or shrink, depending on the amount of light in the room; from time to time he put a few drops of warm water in her dry eyes. Her sunken chest slowly moved up and down, the only sign of life.

Worthy walked outside into the still, snowy night and relieved his bladder beneath a pin oak, planted as a sapling when he and Willa first came to the farm. Now it was taller than the house. A fox screamed once in the distance; it sounded like a woman in distress — an omen of bad luck on its way, his mother would have said. Worthy stood on the back porch with his pipe, drawing and blowing smoke until the fire was gone. He tapped out the ashes against his shoe and put the pipe in his bib pocket.

He walked slowly through the kitchen, climbed the steps to the bedroom and picked up a pillow — one of the two pillows Willa had stuffed with downy duck feathers for their honeymoon bed.

Descending the steps slowly, Worthy crossed the room to where Willa was lying. He hesitated only a second. "I love you, Willa." He bent down and lightly kissed her cool lips. Then he held the pillow over her face, gently, until her sunken chest ceased to move. Once again he bent down close to her face, as if expecting her to speak, then tossed the pillow into a corner. Exhausted, Worthy fell into a chair and contemplated his dead wife.

With no one to count, the mantel clock ticked off the seconds in silence. Finally, Worthy spoke.

"I kissed you, by God," he said, "full on the mouth. I hadn't did that since we courted. And right after I took the pillow off your face, I could of swore I seen your lips move. Hell, I don't know. All I know is I leaned my ear close, and you whispered " 'Fifty-six.' "

WORTHY SAT ALL NIGHT IN THE CHAIR, while an ice storm pelted the snow. Willa's eyes remained open; Worthy found himself talking to her at greater length than when she was alive.

"Willa, you know Cappy's spending the night with his boss? It ain't for me to allow or disallow, he's near growed. But knowing would have killed you quicker than any pillow;

you liked to worry we wasn't raising him right. Jesus, I miss you already, Willa."

"I bet you're up there counting stars this very minute."

Sadly, Worthy went to the phone and rang up Bum.

WORTHY TOOK HIS TIME GOING THROUGH WILLA'S THINGS the next morning. In the way of dresses, there weren't many to choose from; she never was a clotheshorse. But toward the back of the closet he found a black dress that she had worn only once — when Chastity died. The weather's cold for them short sleeves, he thought, but it's the best I can do. He found clean underwear, a pink slip, heavy stockings to hide her varicose veins, and black shoes with sensible heels. By the time he carried the bundle downstairs, Franklin Linder was in the front room waiting, a look of appropriate sympathy on his face.

"I'm sorry to learn of your loss," Franklin said, holding out an icy hand. "And don't worry yourself, I'll be easy with her."

"Before you go, there's a delicate problem I'm bound to bring up," said Worthy. He lowered his voice. "In all the years we was man and wife, I never saw — you know — what parts I was dealing with. After the stroke, when it become necessary I washed her without looking. So when you do what you have to do, I'd greatly appreciate if you'd keep them parts covered."

"Being married myself, I understand perfectly. Ladies who go through my establishment are afforded every courtesy," consoled the undertaker.

"One other thing," Worthy said, as they loaded Willa

inside the hearse. "When she's laid out, I want her eyes left open."

"That's highly unusual. Those who come to view might be offended."

"Offended or not, that's the way it's to be."

Worthy stood by the gate until the hearse was out of sight. As he was walking back toward the house, Cappy turned into the lane. The old Chevy slipped from one side to the other, its four bald tires unable to get traction on the ice. It slid to a stop barely missing the fence.

Cappy guessed the truth immediately. "Did Ma take a sudden turn?"

"You might say that."

"If only I'd been here —" Without finishing his thought, Cappy went upstairs to his room and slammed the door shut. First the stroke and now this, he thought. It's like she died twice! He started to count the string of tragedies that had begun nineteen years earlier with Chastity, then caught himself. "Ma, I know nothing would please you more than if I keep the counting tradition going," he said to the empty room, "but I never was good at ciphers."

He pulled his private box from under the bed and touched each treasure: childhood gifts from Tick, a red scarf Willa had knitted, the letter from Asbury Wollums saying he had won the eighth-grade essay contest, Chastity's theme paper and the school picture from 1922. After one last look, he carried the box outside to the trash barrel and set fire to it. The box and contents flared for a moment, then settled down to smolder. He watched until only ashes remained.

Suddenly aware of what he had done, Cappy dug through the warm ashes to see if anything had escaped the flames, but it was too late. One moment of youthful anger and grief — perhaps an unconscious attempt to get even with them all for leaving him — had taken away tangible memories of Chastity, Tick, Willa. He would regret the irrational act for the rest of his life. Cappy returned to his room and tried to draw a likeness of Chastity before her face faded from his mind's eye.

THE MORNING OF WILLA'S FUNERAL, Cappy had heard nothing from Beany. He had hoped that Beany would play "Rock of Ages" at the service. Several times he had called the Ozbun house, but Mrs. Ozbun would say simply, "Bean is not available." Twice he stopped by the house and knocked, but no one came to the door. Cappy found himself worried and angry. Where was his best friend when he needed him so much? Hadn't Beany said at the March of Dimes Dance that he had come home on leave to surprise Cappy?

Also absent was Tick. Cappy and Worthy's hope was that he would hear the death report on the radio and show up at the last minute. Cappy and Worthy sat in the front row with a seat saved for Tick.

THE CHURCH WAS FULL TO OVERFLOWING. Brother Beams began the funeral sermon by pointing out the happy occasion that had brought the mourners together. "Count your blessings, my friends, for what better way is there to honor this dear departed wife, mother, grandmother and patriot?" He went on to praise God for everything under the sun: new lambs being born, automobiles, the war that was giving young men the opportunity of seeing the world, the ball-bat factory where women were filling in for those brave soldiers. In closing, he lifted his voice and eyes toward the ceiling, as if Willa and God were perched on the light fixture together. "No doubt our Dear Sister is at this very moment counting the many friends who have come to celebrate her passing."

Chapter XXIV

Monday morning, the day after Willa's funeral, Sheriff Perdun arrived at his office early. Remembering a call that had come in the night after the dance, he dug through a stack of papers until he found the message from Lafe Ozbun. The note said that his boy, Bean, had been missing since the dance, but that his car was sitting out front with his Army cap in the back seat. When Bean hadn't come down for dinner that noon, Lafe and Viola figured the boy was overly tired from his trip across the waters and was catching up on his sleep. But when he didn't come down for supper either, Viola went upstairs to check on him. He wasn't in his room and from appearances he hadn't been there to sleep. Lafe went on to say that he had asked around town, but no one had seen Bean. Lafe wanted Sheriff Perdun to look into the matter.

When he first read the note, the sheriff guessed Beany had spent the night with his buddies or a girlfriend and let it go at that. He had put the message aside and had forgotten it.

But now he called in his deputies for an emergency meeting and deputized two extra men to help with the search.

It was friday noon of that same week. Sheriff Perdun was at his desk finishing a piece of Widow Glohr's prize-winning coconut cream cake when Harry Waltrip, the county coroner, walked in. He appeared out of sorts, muttering about not being informed of Willa Giberson's death.

Before his recent retirement to Old Kane, Harry had spent thirty-five years working at a nut-and-bolt factory in East St. Louis where he kept track of every nut and bolt made, who bought them and when, and how many were used for each job. As coroner, Harry searched for clues as diligently as if he were searching employees' pockets for a missing nut.

"If Worthy's wife had been found alongside the roadway or killed by a shotgun, I would have gotten word to you somehow. But mercifully she just quit breathing. Where's the suspicion in that?"

"It sounds like you haven't heard the rumors."

"If I paid attention to every rumor that passes through my ears, I wouldn't get another thing done."

"This particular rumor was told by Bum Hetzel, who claims the Giberson woman was murdered by having a pillow placed over her face."

Sheriff Perdun laughed out loud at Harry's gullibility, a real city slicker. "It's plain to see you're a newcomer to Old Kane, Harry. Otherwise you'd know there isn't a bigger storyteller in all of Greene County than Worthy Giberson, with the second biggest being Bum Hetzel. Bum no doubt told that tale to liven up a conversation in Pick's Store."

"Pick's Store *is* where the story first came to light, but it was said Bum's voice cracked when he related the details. What did Doc Potter write down as the cause of death?"

"Some fancy words that mean her heart stopped."

Harry left the sheriff's office and drove to the Giberson farm; some serious questions needed to be asked. He found Worthy inside the cowbarn helping Shag Kallal scoop steaming manure.

"A couple more scoops and I'll leave the rest for Shag. You can set and wait for me in the kitchen. Help yourself to the coffeepot."

By the time Harry was settled at the kitchen table, Worthy was stomping snow from his boots onto the back porch. He entered the warm kitchen and tossed his coat and cap in a corner. "There's nothing I like more than a cold winter's morning and the feel of a shovel in my hands," he said.

"I prefer summer, myself," Harry said, "although the summer sun's not kind to the bodies I come in contact with. Now the reason for my visit . . . I'm here to talk about your recently deceased wife. What about the incident with the pillow?"

Worthy hesitated. "Who said anything about a pillow?"

"Bum Hetzel. He said that your wife was smothered with her pillow while you were otherwise occupied. Is that what happened?"

"I ain't one to dispute what another man says." Worthy squirmed in his chair, crossing first one leg and then the other.

"Does that mean you're substantiating his story?"

"It means I'd best be getting back to the manure. Shag's burdened with a weak back. I don't want him to get down from shoveling the entire barn."

"I want you to know I'm not at all satisfied here," Harry said.

OTHER THAN THE FUNERAL, Worthy had not been off the home place since Willa's stroke. In five months, nothing had changed except the season. Snowy fields had taken the place of tassled rows of corn; and with nothing to graze on, cattle huddled together against the blustery wind. Worthy found Bum in the kitchen trimming his toenails and listening to *Lorenzo Jones* on the radio.

"Jesus Christ, Bum! What was you thinking of, telling that story about Willa being smothered by an intruder."

Bum turned down the radio. "I was only taking measures in case questioning was put forth."

"Thanks to you and your fool storying, Harry Waltrip is putting forth a good many questions. Without that twister of yours, Willa's passing would of gone unnoticed!"

"I was only looking out for you," Bum said. "In your condition, you was likely to say anything. Cappy's lost two mothers. He don't need to lose his pa, too."

AS EACH DAY PASSED with no word from Beany, Cappy's concern grew. He drove around the country asking if anyone had seen a lost soldier, but no one had. It was as if Beany had disintegrated. Every morning on his way to the newspaper, Cappy stopped by the courthouse, always asking the same question of the weary sheriff. "Are you making any headway?"

"I'm stymied, Cappy," the sheriff told him. "In all my years of sheriffing, this beats anything I've come up against. The Ozbuns both say they looked out the window about midnight the night of the dance and the family car was parked under the maple tree, right where it was supposed to be —"

Cappy knew the story by heart, but he let the sheriff ramble on.

"Could it be you've got a hunch you aren't letting out?" Cappy asked finally.

"Nothing for the newspaper. My first hunch was that the Woosley Twins figured in this some way. The incident could be a simple case of kidnapping — I always figured they kidnapped Dinghie Varble back in '39 for sport."

"It may not do any good," Cappy said, "but I want to do some poking around on my own."

"Just don't get your hopes up for a happy outcome."

The telephone rang and the sheriff answered. He listened for a minute, then hung up the receiver. "That was Chief Chissum out west of Old Kane. He was down working in his gulley and came across a body. I'm heading that way now. You can follow in your own car."

Cappy's blood turned as cold as the day. He shivered all the way to the gulley.

Chief Chissum was waiting at the gulley entrance when the two men arrived. "He's hard to spot if you don't know just where he's at."

Cappy and the sheriff followed Chief; the body was lying face down in a frozen snowdrift. Cappy looked at it in anguish. Who else would be wearing a uniform of the U.S. Army but Beany?

The sheriff avoided Cappy's eyes. "Did you determine the identity?" he asked Chief.

"It's Beany Ozbun, all right. I prized up his head for a look, but let it drop back so as not to disturb the scene."

Since the big snow the day of the March of Dimes Dance and the ice storm that followed, temperatures had remained below zero. The body was frozen solid in ice and it took the three men to pry it from the ground and turn it over.

"Looks like the fall caused his nose to bleed," the sheriff said. The snow beneath Beany's face was the color of pink carnations.

Cappy let the tears come. Beany's frozen face was curiously sad as if he regretted his best friend's pain. Cappy found himself crying out, "Piano players don't have enemies!"

NEWS OF THE TRAGEDY settled around Old Kane like a shroud. No one could think of a motive for murder, but everyone agreed it was a shame that Beany had made it through the war safe, only to meet with such an end in his own backyard.

Worthy tried his best to console Cappy, but he would have none of it. "Save your breath, Pa. There's nothing you can say to make things better. Just don't tell me he's in that 'better place' alongside Ma!"

Worthy recognized the anger, having been through all its stages himself.

Min offered Cappy the week off, but he showed up early each morning and stayed all day. Work was his daytime comfort; nights he spent in Min's arms.

THE FIRST EVENING OF THE WAKE, Cappy went expecting to have one last look at his friend, but the Ozbuns had asked to have the coffin closed — the first such request Franklin Linder had in a lifetime of wakes.

"G. I. Jive" blared from the jukebox next door at Mundy's Cafe; pool balls clicked together; somebody told a joke. Cappy wondered why Franklin had chosen the middle of Main Street for his funeral parlor. He was glad Willa's wake had been in her own front room among the things she loved: her matching overstuffed furniture, the maroon rug, her collection of cups and saucers. . . .

When Cappy attempted to console Beany's mother, Viola lost her composure. "Oh, yes!" she said, putting a handkerchief to her lips. "Bean will be going away to college soon and study music."

Goosebumps covered Cappy's arms at Viola Ozbun's chilling words. He had seen the same aberrant behavior in Mary Lee Margeson — the young mother who carried around a rubber baby. Viola was denying that her child was dead. Although Cappy had never liked Beany's mother, when he saw how she had aged during the past week — her eyes dull, her face sagging — he softened toward her.

AT ELEVEN O'CLOCK, the undertaker began encouraging people to leave, shooing them out the door as if they were children out past their bedtime. Cappy remained behind, until he could hear Franklin in the back room closing down for the night, whistling as he always did after a successful wake. But Cappy could not leave.

He lifted the top of Beany's coffin and looked inside. Beany was dressed in his Army uniform, a sober look on his face, his dark curly hair cropped close. "One thing about Army barbers," Beany had said after basic training, "they make sure you don't come out looking like a girl."

A worn copy of Chopin's *Fantasie Impromptu* rested alongside Beany; even in death Beany was a classical pianist to his mother. Cappy sighed. Beany would have as much use for that music as a kid for marbles. But who was to say for sure? The Egyptian pharaohs thought differently. Suddenly Cappy reached in his back pocket and gave Beany his pocketknife. Beany had often admired the pearl-handled knife, a gift from Worthy on Cappy's sixth birthday. "I'll will it to you," Cappy had joked.

After the funeral, Cappy drove to Carrollton to see Min and stay the night in her blue bedroom. She listened to story after story of boyhood adventures he and Beany had shared, until he fell asleep at her breast. Several times during the night she tried to turn over to find a more comfortable position, but each time she moved, Cappy clamped his mouth harder to her.

Since beany ozbun's death, Pick's regulars showed up early to get a seat near the stove, hoping for some reliable hearsay to sweeten their coffee. In view of the tragedy, Pick was handing out full cups of coffee, rationing be damned.

Worthy, back at his accustomed place once more, had been given a royal welcome; each man vigorously shook his hand and clapped his back. Pick dusted out Worthy's coffee cup and filled it to the brim. "While you've been gone, no one but you has drank from your cup."

"I'm obliged", Worthy said, at ease for the first time in five months. "This day was a long time coming." He took a deep, slow drink of the strong brew. Pick's coffee had never tasted so good.

Talk ranged from FDR's possible fourth term to the banning of horse races for the duration. Finally, Pick got around to the subject on everyone's mind.

"Right about now, I wager poor Beany Ozbun is wishing he'd stayed in Germany where it was safe. And Cappy, how's he taking it?"

"Like you'd expect of Cappy", Worthy said. "He's not one to let on what he's feeling; he keeps it all inside. When he ain't at the newspaper or Min Wollums's place, he's setting in the house thinking. He won't say what about."

While drayton hunt was cleaning the inside of his Moon, he found a pink celluloid Kewpie doll, no bigger than his thumb, lying on the back floorboard. "What the hell is this?" he said out loud. Then he remembered that the twins had been in his car. "It must've fell out of that fool George's pocket." He was about to toss it away when he changed his mind. "I'll have a little fun with that dumb prick, a growed man carrying around a doll. He'll have to set up and beg before he gets this back!" He tied a piece of twine around the doll's neck and hung it over the rearview mirror where George was sure to see it — like dangling a bone in front of a hungry dog.

When he finished with the inside of the car, he gently soaped and rinsed the outside. With one of Mae's tea towels, he dried and polished until the royal blue finish glowed. He stood back and admired his handiwork. What a beauty, he thought. If only life was as untroublesome as his car.

Chapter XXV

$\mathcal{N}$ever had the Greene County Courthouse been so crowded as it was for the inquest into Beany Ozbun's death. Every chair was taken, with people standing in the back and around both sides. The jury filed in, eliciting murmurs of admiration from the crowd. At the coroner's insistence, each man was wearing a suit coat and tie. The group included Shag Kallal, Pick and Mayor Dinghie Varble.

There as a reporter, Cappy sat in the front row. He saved a seat for Min, his editor. The Ozbuns had chosen not to attend. As the proceedings were about to begin, Drayton Hunt and the Woosley Twins slipped in.

The coroner read from the official coroner's handbook: "Gentlemen of the jury and other interested persons. This inquest is for the purpose of looking into a death that has occurred in Greene County — that of Beany Ozbun, recently returned soldier in the Army of the United States. Beany Ozbun was pronounced dead at the scene by myself,

Harry W. Waltrip, Coroner of Greene County, State of Illinois. Keep in mind this is neither a criminal nor civil investigation but merely an inquest into the manner and cause of this death. After all the evidence is presented, it will then be the duty of the jury to determine whether the death was from suicide, homicide, accident or natural causes, and whether blame should be placed on anyone. Members of the jury may ask questions of the witnesses." He laid the book aside.

"My first witness in this inquest is Chief Chissum. Please state your name, address and occupation."

"Chief Chissum, Rural Route, Old Kane, gulley caretaker."

"Is 'Chief' your real name?"

"I go by 'Chief' because my grandpa was a full-blooded Sioux Indian."

"Thank you. Now please tell what you found in the gulley on January 28."

"Well, it was eight days after the March of Dimes Dance and I had went to the gulley to see if anything of value had been discarded. The right front tire of my pickup was so thin you could see the air bubbling inside and I was on the lookout for a replacement — you know how scarce a rubber tire is these days with all the rubber going to the war. I was about to take my leave when I seen something on the ground close to the remains of Slip Stringer's old silver Buick. I got down for a better look, and that's when I seen it was a human being's remains. It was Beany Ozbun."

Next, Sheriff Perdun eased his large frame into the small chair. He was perspiring heavily; testifying made him as nervous as a tight-wire walker. He wiped his face and neck with a large bandanna, more determined than ever to find another line of work. Methodically and without emotion, he recounted the events at Chief's gulley.

"What is your opinion as to how Beany Ozbun died?" the coroner asked.

"You yourself said it was from exposure. That's what you wrote on the temporary death certificate."

"Yes, it would be impossible for a person to remain outside in freezing weather without suffering from exposure."

The coroner appeared to be mulling the sheriff's words as if they had just occurred to him. He read the instructions: "Gentlemen of the jury, this constitutes all the evidence. It will now be your duty to deliberate on the findings and determine whether this death was from homicide, suicide, accident or natural causes, and whether blame should be placed on anyone. You gentlemen may now retire to the next room and deliberate."

As foreman, Dinghie Varble sat at the head of the rectangular table. Notebooks and pencils were provided for jurors; when the time came, each man would write his decision and hand the paper to Dinghie, who would tally the votes.

"Well, fellas, let's get to the business at hand," he said.

"It wasn't likely suicide," said Shag Kallal. "A man set on killing himself can find any number of ways more pleasurable than freezing to death."

"We can throw out suicide altogether," Dinghie said. "From what I viewed at the March of Dimes Dance, Beany Ozbun was planning some good times with Cappy. That leaves murder and accident. Fellas, here are the facts as we know them. Beany Ozbun was missing for eight days. Then he was found in the gulley face down. Sounds like murder to me."

"That's not necessarily so," said Pick. "It's fairly commonplace for a man to get lost in zero weather and freeze to death by accident."

As the courthouse clock struck ten p.m., the jury returned to the courtroom. Half the audience was asleep, the other half had gone home to bed.

"Foreman Varble, have you reached a verdict?" the coroner asked.

"We deem his death to be from accident," Dinghie replied, looking appropriately solemn and professional, "and here's our chain of reasoning. We know Beany left the March of Dimes Dance. We figured he was tired out from his trip across the waters and got drowsy and thought to go home. When he was driving past Chief's Gulley he felt a nature call and stopped to relieve himself. Most generally, when the thermometer hits below zero, the cold adds to a body's feeling of tiredness, so after resting a while on the hood of Slip Stringer's old silver Buick, he went to sleep and rolled onto the ground and never woke up."

"Don't any of you know what the word 'accident' means?" Harry was suddenly sorry he had ever been appointed coroner.

"We're not morons," Dinghie said, indignantly. "Accident means when a man dies but he didn't mean to."

"The jury is excused. Stop by the sheriff's office and collect your pay." All my hours of work down the drain, the coroner thought as he gathered up his papers and left by the back door.

"I'll be around to see you in the morning," Cappy said to the sheriff. Like the coroner, he thought the jury was a bunch of idiots.

"What a fiasco," the sheriff said, as if reading Cappy's mind. "Come early, I need to take the rest of the day off."

Chapter XXVI

By seven o'clock the next morning, the coffee drinkers began drifting into Pick's Store. Worthy and Bum were the first to arrive. Burley Walk, the shell-shocked veteran of World War I, slipped in behind the others; he sat on the floor near the stove reading a *Superman* comic book. As he always did, Worthy saluted Burley.

"If calamities keep turning up, it looks like I'll have to invest in more chairs," Pick said. "The least you loafers could do is carry your own seat." He brought in a large crate from the storeroom and dropped it next to the stove.

"Is that any way to talk to your best customers?" Worthy teased.

"Let's keep things congenial, Worthy," Pick said. "By the way, I've expanded my stock to include some doodads for the womenfolk, pretties they can set on the sideboard or bureau top. Feel free to make a purchase for the little woman, those of you who've still got one."

Only Burley showed any interest. He walked over to the display shelf and fingered a fancy thimble and a miniature coal-oil lamp with a pink glass globe. He picked up a small celluloid doll and turned it upside down to look at the painted-on panties. "George's got one of these," he said.

Worthy looked Burley's way. "What's that you said, Burley?"

"George lets me play inside his pocket for a nickel. That's when I felt his doll. I seen it, too." He giggled.

"George who?" Worthy asked, his heart beginning to race.

"The George that's got the twin," Burley said, sniffing the doll.

"Ain't that like Willa's doll?" Bum asked Worthy.

"It's something like it, only hers was littler. I won Willa's doll at the fair when we was courting. I give it to her in place of a wedding ring, that being solely her own idea."

"I always puzzled at her not wearing no wedding ring like other wives," Bum said. "I chalked it up as you being too stingy to buy her one."

"Another case of you chalking wrong." Worthy was out the door.

"Look at this," Pick said as he picked up Worthy's cup. "Damned if he didn't leave several good swallows. It isn't like Worthy to not drink every drop."

When cappy came home from the paper, Worthy had supper waiting: fried potatoes, fried side meat, slices of fried bread, all cooked in last year's strong lard. But Cappy didn't have an appetite. All he could think of was Beany.

"I heard some news today that'll make you prick up your ears," Worthy said as he set the food on the table and took his usual chair. "You remember that Kewpie of your Ma's?"

"I remember. You wanted to bury it with her." To be polite, Cappy fixed a fried potato sandwich and put it on his plate. "Did you find it? Ma's Kewpie?"

"Could be. According to Burley Walk, a doll like your Ma's is riding in George Woosley's pocket."

"How do you know it's hers? Kewpie dolls all look alike to me."

"I won't know for sure till I look it over, but I've got a gut feeling it's hers. Before I give it to your ma, I scratched her and my initials on the bottom of its feet. Women like them kind of touches. You might want to keep that in mind when you get a woman of your own."

Suddenly Cappy was interested. "Wait, Pa, if George has Ma's doll, that means he's been here in the house."

"So it seems. Thinking on it makes my skin crawl."

"He must've sneaked in the house to rob, got spooked when he saw Ma's eyes were open, and ended up smothering her, like Bum has claimed. And I thought all the time Bum was storying."

Worthy nearly dropped his fork. "Hold up, now, the twins has been pranksters over the years, even into a robbery here and there, but I don't see either one of them capable of rendering . . ."

"Maybe not on their own. But what if they were in the company of someone who *was* capable of murder?"

"First thing tomorrow morning I'm driving to Woosleys' to look at that doll," Worthy said. "If it turns out to be your

Ma's, I'm calling Jesse Perdun and having the twins both hauled off to jail for stealing. You never see one of them boys without the other so it stands to reason Ralph was in on it."

"If George has the doll, he wouldn't show it to you, Pa. There's a better chance of getting it back if the sheriff confronts him." Cappy jumped up from the table and ran out the door before Worthy could present another argument.

"You didn't finish your feed," Worthy called after him.

"No time, Pa," he called back. "I aim to talk to Min before seeing the sheriff. And I may stay the night."

"Give the lady my regards —" but Cappy was already out of hearing.

Worthy scooped Cappy's sandwich onto his own plate and devoured it, food having regained its taste with a vengeance. Contented, he sat back and patted his expanding belly.

BY THE TIME CAPPY ARRIVED AT MIN'S, his plan was well in mind, but she would take some convincing. He told her about Burley and the doll and his suspicion concerning the Woosley Twins — providing the doll turned out to be Willa's. "There's no proof of any of this, so as a trap, I want to write a phony article for the front page, maybe have some notices printed to post around the county, and then sit back and see who takes the bait."

"Why doesn't the sheriff just confront George? Wouldn't that be quicker?"

"George would say Burley dreamed the whole thing, and then he'd throw the doll away."

"But even if George did steal Willa's doll, what does that have to do with Beany's death? I can't see the connection."

"The connection is purely of my own making. I know the twins left the March of Dimes Dance at intermission and went to Oettle's for a beer, and after the dance Drayton joined them. It's possible Drayton had Beany's murder in mind before leaving the dance, as mad as he looked, and he needed somebody along to help. But there's more."

"This is as complicated as one of Az's novels," Min said, "but go on."

"What if Drayton and the twins were driving by our house and the twins got an idea for a prank? I can see Drayton allowing them their fun, even joining them. Once they all three got inside the house and Drayton noticed Ma's eyes were open, to be on the safe side he smothered her. On the way out of the house, George picked up Ma's Kewpie doll. What do you think?"

Min thought for a minute. "Even if your theory is true, proving it won't be easy. But I'll stand behind whatever you want to print. And I'm sorry about your friend, Cappy."

Cappy's eyes filled with tears. He turned his head so Min wouldn't see.

After sheriff perdun read the proposed notice, Cappy explained his theory.

"And your pa knows without question it's Willa's doll?"

"He'll be sure once he looks at it. Before giving it to her, he marked it in a special way."

"Jesus, I thought Harry was a mile off-base questioning Worthy about Willa's death. Now it appears he had the right idea. Getting our hands on that doll would be a good start toward finding proof."

"A lot depends on what happens when the paper comes out next Friday. The notices will go up first."

"Even if you're right, Cappy, your plan may not work. Drayton Hunt is a mean son of a bitch, but he's no fool."

"I'm counting on the Woosley Twins to be fool enough for the three of them."

REWARD OFFERED FOR MISSING DOLL

The Greene County Sheriff's Office is offering the generous reward of $25.00 for a pink Kewpie doll lost in the vicinity of Old Kane. Anyone finding such a doll should bring it to the Sheriff's Office for verification, and to collect the reward if it turns out to be the missing doll. No questions asked.

SHERIFF PERDUN WAS PLAGUED from morning to night with people lined up outside his door waiting to bring in dolls for inspection, from a homemade Raggedy Ann to a Shirley Temple doll with yellow spit curls. Each person hoped his or her doll would resemble the missing doll enough to collect the reward.

"I don't know how much longer I can tolerate them damned dolls," the sheriff told Cappy, "and so far I haven't laid eyes on the Wooseleys."

"Give them time. They're a little slow when it comes to reading."

IT WAS NINE SATURDAY NIGHT. Ralph and George were in their usual booth at Oettle's having one last beer before starting home. They had come from the show, disappointed with the picture, *Madame Curie.*

"What a waste of two bits!" Ralph grumbled. "I never would of went in the first place, but you said it was about a madam and her dance hall girls."

"That's what Dinghie hisself told me. I thought he'd ought to know if anybody would."

"He never watches a picture — he's too busy watching to see that nobody slips in without paying. Dinghie took one look at your dumb kisser and knew you'd swallow whatever he fed you."

"You can go to hell!" George said.

"And you with me!" Since the March of Dimes Dance, both men had short fuses.

Ralph picked up a copy of the *Democrat-Republican Patriot,* left in the booth by a previous customer. "Listen to this," he said, the flare-up forgotten. He read the notice of the missing doll out loud. "I sure as hell could put that twenty-five bucks to healthy use. Trouble is finding a dollie to fit the bill."

"Could be I've got such a dollie."

"What would a growed man be doing with a dollie?"

"Could be I come across one and hung onto it for safe-keeping."

"Could be you keep it hid under the covers at night so you can rub it on that little pecker of yours!"

"You can go to hell!"

"And you with me!" Ralph read the reward notice again. "If you do have such a dollie, George, it wouldn't cost nothing to take it by Jesse's office and see if it might be a match. Where'd you find it anyway?"

"Setting on Worthy Giberson's hallway table."

"Jesus! Well, that puts the kibosh on showing it to the sheriff. You'd better throw the damned thing away before it gets the both of us in a peck of trouble. Where is it now?"

"Right here in my overhalls." George reached in his pocket, and began pulling out keepsakes — a rabbit's foot, an eight-pager, a fish scaler — but the doll was not there. "Shit, I could of swore I had it!" He turned his pockets wrongside out. "I recall showing it to Burley Walk the day of the March of Dimes Dance."

"Why did you do a fool trick like that?" Ralph asked. "I can hear him blabbing it all over town."

"Shit, Burley don't remember nothing from one day to the next."

"That's true enough," Ralph agreed. "Maybe Ma took it out when she washed."

"This is my new pair; they ain't due for a wash. Jesus, somebody's picked my damned pocket!"

"Maybe that somebody done us a favor," Ralph said.

WHILE HE WAS DRIVING TO TOWN, Drayton came across one of the notices tacked to a telephone pole. He stopped to read it. The lost doll sounded like the one George had left in the back seat of his car. Drayton laughed. I bet the poor bastard's tearing the house and barn apart looking for that doll. Drayton considered turning it in himself; he could use the twenty-five dollars as well as George, but he decided against it. He left the tiny pink doll hanging in his Moon without another thought.

"WELL, CAPPY," Sheriff Perdun said, a few days later, "your notices dredged up everybody in Greene County *but* the Woosley Twins."

"Couldn't you bring them in for questioning because of what Burley said? They might let something slip."

"There's always the chance Burley was having a delusion that day, but I'd be interested in hearing what those two have to say for themselves."

"Then you'll pick them up?"

"First thing tomorrow."

SHERIFF PERDUN SENT HIS CHIEF DEPUTY to bring in the twins. By nine o'clock, the two redheaded men were sitting in the sheriff's cramped office. Cappy was there, presumably for the newspaper.

"What's this about, Sheriff?" Ralph asked. "We was minding our own business helping Ma kill chickens when Specs drove up."

"Word has come to me that you boys are in possession of some stolen property."

"We give up thievery a long time back, Sheriff," George said.

"According to Burley Walk, one of you carries a Kewpie doll in your pocket that once belonged to Willa Giberson," the sheriff said. "Is that true?"

"Now, Sheriff," Ralph forced a laugh, "what would a

growed man be doing with a Kewpie doll? Besides, you can't lay store in what Burley says, poor devil."

"Go ahead and feel inside my pockets, all of them," George offered. "I guarantee you won't find no dollie."

"Burley may be a little off-center, but that shell-shock didn't affect his eyes." The sheriff sat back and lit a cigar, enjoying the moment. He would let them sweat before continuing the questioning.

"You know, I've been thinking," he said at last. "There may be more to this than the simple theft of a doll." He proceeded to tell Cappy's theory, ending with the suggestion that they had been in Worthy's house the night of the dance and had stolen the doll. "Well, boys, what have you got to say for yourselves?"

"We've got you there, Sheriff," George said, laughing too loud. "The night of the dance we was —"

"We was having a beer at Oettle's," Ralph interrupted, "and then we went straight on home."

"Were you drinking alone that night, or did someone join you? Maybe Drayton Hunt?"

"He did come in for a beer," Ralph said. "We set and conversed about the dance and the snowstorm."

"Later that night you were seen riding around town in that fancy motorcar of his. Is that right?" (A lie could sometimes help get at the truth.)

"Hell, no, we didn't go no place with him, Sheriff," George said. "He won't let nobody close to that motorcar, let alone ride in it."

"Well maybe we'd better pick up the gentleman and see if he backs up your story."

Persuading Drayton to go to the courthouse was easier than the sheriff had anticipated. "Sure, I'll go," Drayton said, "but I'll get there under my own steam."

"WHAT'S THIS ABOUT, JESSE?" Drayton addressed the sheriff as he lit a cigarette and took a couple of puffs.

"I won't detain you longer than needs be, I know you're a busy man. To make a long story short, Ralph and George Woosley say you can provide them with an alibi for a particular night in question. They're claiming that following the March of Dimes Dance, they went for a late-night ride in your Moon." (Another lie looking for the truth.)

"What have them two got theirselves into now?" Drayton chuckled good-naturedly. "Them boys is real cards."

"Just answer the question." Jesse Perdun was feeling the beginnings of a headache.

"Jesse, before I answer, let me first interject my condolences to Cappy here on losing both his sweet mamas."

"Don't get off the track, Hunt. Did you take the Woosley Twins for a ride after the March of Dimes Dance, or didn't you?" His headache was advancing to the pounding stage and the sheriff felt his left eye twitch.

"Jesse, nothing would make me prouder than being able to help my fellow human beings, but my conscience won't allow. I did see both boys at the dance, but as I recall they took off at intermission or thereabout. I hung around till the last song was played, not wanting to appear rude, and then after a quick beer at Oettle's, I went direct home to set with my own dear mama. She's been under the weather of late. Sick as she was, nothing would do her but I should go to the dance and help buy an iron lung for some poor cripple."

"Did you happen across the twins at Oettle's?"

"Let me think — I believe I did. Yes, they was there setting in their usual booth. Fact is, I joined them while I finished my beer. And then I drove straight home to be with my mama, like I said. I'm only sorry I couldn't been of more help." He tipped his hat to Cappy, and started to get up.

"Hold on, Hunt, we're not through here. It's come to light you might know something about what went on in Chief's Gulley."

Drayton dropped his cigarette on the floor and ground it out with his heel. "I suppose them half-wits told that lie, too?"

"Maybe yes, maybe no."

"All I know about Chief's Gulley is this." Drayton shifted in his chair. "It's where Beany Ozbun met his maker."

Sheriff Perdun knew he had nothing to hold Drayton on.

"THAT JOKER IS GUILTY of something." Cappy was disappointed with the outcome of the questioning.

"I agree with you, but if we went into court, we'd fall flat on our face," said the sheriff.

"But what about Burley seeing the doll?" Cappy had counted heavily on Burley's story.

"You know as well as I do how far Burley's testimony would get in the courtroom. We'll have to try a different route." Sheriff Perdun fished around in his desk drawer for his Bayers.

THE FOLLOWING ARTICLE APPEARED in the *Democrat-Republican Patriot*'s February 18th, 1944 issue:

AN INTERVIEW WITH MR. PORTIER WHITLOCK
by Cappy Giberson

It was my good fortune to interview Mr. Portier Whitlock, a respected criminologist and psychologist from Chicago, Illinois, regarding the mind and how it works, and why some minds turn to crime.

According to Mr. Whitlock, by the time a boy begins first grade, his mind is set for the remainder of his life. Sometimes his mind turns bad because of not having a father.

Mr. Whitlock went on to say that the criminal mind has nothing to do with intelligence, or how successful the criminal is at his chosen crime. Even if he has the mind of a genius, he may become careless and leave behind a clue as large as a glove or as small as a hair from his head. It is possible for a clue to remain undetected for months. Mr. Whitlock said he has solved many crimes by getting down on his hands and knees and using a magnifying glass.

I asked Mr. Whitlock if he believes the criminal mind can be corrected. He does not think so. Therefore he advises parents to make sure their children's minds are set in the right direction in the first place.

Late Saturday night, Drayton read the paper at Mundy's Café.

"Cappy Giberson must deem me to be a moron," he said to the waitress, "him and his shitty tricks."

"What tricks would that be honey?"

"Oh, that interview with some bigshot named Whitlock, for one. Cappy Giberson's so transparent a blind man could see through him."

"I read the interview but I didn't see any trick," the waitress said, touching his hand as she passed him a free doughnut. She was hoping for a ride in his Moon.

"Christ! Do I have to draw you a picture? Cappy thought to plant a doubt in the killer's mind about maybe leaving a clue behind, thinking the killer would revisit the scene and try and retrieve the clue before somebody else found it. And that half-assed sheriff would no doubt be waiting in the bushes with a pair of handcuffs."

But Drayton *was* pleased to note that while Chief's Gulley was watched day and night, in the first few months, one by one the sheriff and his deputies found something else to do. Sheriff Perdun was the last to give up the surveillance in favor of an evening with Widow Glohr and her warm mincemeat pie.

And so Drayton Hunt became the most visible man in Old Kane. On Saturday nights when Main Street was crowded with farm families in town to do their weekly shopping and see a picture show, he would grin and tip his hat to each lady, young or old. And if there weren't too many customers in Oettle's Tavern, he would buy drinks for every man there.

Chapter XXVII

The truth was, after leaving the March of Dimes Dance, Drayton *had* driven to Oettle's Tavern. Buck was trying to close, but the Woosley Twins were refusing to leave. And now Drayton Hunt would add to Buck's worriment.

"Give me a beer," Drayton said, striding up to the bar, a cigarette hanging from his mouth.

"Sure thing." Buck forced a polite smile. "I'll be open another fifteen minutes," he said as he handed over the beer. "It's already past my closing."

"I'll let you know when it's closing time, old man." Drayton joined the twins in the back booth. "Jesus Christ, you look like a couple of hoboes just off a Burlington freight. No wonder I didn't see you on the dance floor."

"We wasn't all that keen on dancing," George said.

"I wasn't in the mood, either," Drayton said. He took a long slow drink of the warm beer. "That was a poor excuse for a dance. And that colored man playing the drums — it was enough to make me puke."

"He could sure drum, though," Ralph said.

"That ain't the point," Drayton said. "There's some things in this life that ought not to be. And another thing that galled me — that soldier showing up."

"What soldier?" Ralph asked.

"You'd know what soldier if you hadn't run off early like a couple of coyotes." Drayton tipped the bottle to get the last drop. "It was Lafe Ozbun's boy, that sissy that plays the piano. You'd of thought he was General MacArthur the way everybody was making over him."

"Him and Cappy Giberson are thick as thorns," George said. "Do you reckon they're getting under the covers together?"

George's words made Drayton pause. Could it be that a boy of his blood had been persuaded to go down that unspeakable slippery route?

"Cappy ain't no prissy," he said, his words sharp. "He's a man all the way. Just ask that newspaper woman in Carrollton. From all accounts, he burns up the road going back and forth to her bed."

"Maybe Cappy goes *both* roads —"

That was the final insult. Drayton shouted in George's face. "Maybe you two bozos are dicking each other! You've both got the mouth for it! Another beer over here, Buck!

"I've had enough of you two morons spouting off for one night," Drayton went back to the twins, "so keep your yaps shut while I enjoy my drink." He was angry that he had let them get to him with their insinuations about Cappy. He brooded through two more beers with no words passed among the three men. Finally Drayton wiped his mouth on his sleeve and stood up. "It's closing time, Buck!"

"You owe me two bits."

"I don't owe you nothing. Them beers was flat as George Woosley's head." He stepped outside into the still, snowy night. There were no cars on the street except his Moon — parked beneath Old Kane's lone street lamp. "Christ, this town's a tomb. You boys want to join me in a little good-natured fun?"

Apparently Drayton was over his snit. The twins were surprised the way he had gone off at their teasing of Cappy, but they knew better than to ask.

"What kind of fun?" Ralph asked.

"I ain't decided yet. Help me clean the snow off my Moon and we'll be on our way."

"How about a little bushwacking?" George said, as they got under way down Main Street.

"Who'd be out on a night like this?" Ralph asked.

"We're out, ain't we?" George said.

"I hope to hell we don't get stuck," Ralph said. "This street's as bad as I've seen it, and the snow's still coming down."

"My Moon will take me anyplace I want to go." Drayton gently stroked the dashboard as if it were a woman's thigh. As they came to the school where the dance had been, Drayton noticed two cars parked at the side of the gymnasium. "What have we got here? That sure as hell looks like Lafe

Ozbun's car and Worthy Giberson's," he said. "My curiosity's up. Maybe we'll just set here for a while. I've got all night."

Drayton backed half a block from the school where he could watch the two parked cars. He turned off the headlamps but left the engine idling. He lit a cigarette and leaned back to wait. The snow had stopped.

A few minutes later, Worthy's car left and turned onto the road leading to Carrollton. Drayton watched as a shadowy figure got into the other car, then stepped out and started fiddling with the hood.

Drayton drove the Moon to within a few inches of the Ozbun car's front bumper. He left the headlamps on. "Having car trouble?" he asked.

"I had it running but then it died and wouldn't start again," Beany said, looking up at the tall man's hardened face. "I don't know anything about cars. Maybe the battery's dead; I couldn't get it to turn the engine over. I guess Pa's rattletrap's seen better days."

"Oh, she ain't a bad old car," Drayton said. "Maybe she just needs a *man's* touch." The twins laughed.

"Pa and I'll come back in the morning and see if we can get it going," Beany said. "Anyway, much obliged for stopping to help." He started to walk away.

"Hold on, General," Drayton said, flourishing an exaggerated salute. "Truth is, me and the boys never met a sure-enough war hero in the flesh, and when we seen you was having trouble, this seemed like as good a time as any."

Beany caught the subtle change in Drayton's tone. He crossed his arms over his chest and stood his ground in an attempt to hide his sudden fear — a trick the Army had taught him.

"Close up, you look like the same little piano-playing turd you always was." Drayton spit onto the fresh snow. "I'm clearly disappointed, ain't you boys?"

"I was expecting him to have a chest full of medals," George said. He knocked Beany's hat into the snow and laughed.

Beany's uneasiness was growing. "I'd better head home," he said.

"What was you and Worthy's boy up to, setting in the same car so long?" George said. "Did you have your hand in his pants? Or did he have his hand in yours?"

"Move out of my way!"

"When we're good and ready," Drayton said. "But since Ralph brought up the issue, here's a warning. Stay the hell away from Cappy Giberson. He ain't the likes of you."

"Cappy's no concern of yours," Beany said.

"That's for me to say. I'm telling you again, stay the hell away from Cappy Giberson! He's already got a girlfriend." The twins guffawed.

"You son of a bitch!" Beany shouted, his fists clenched.

Drayton shoved Beany aside, like a schoolyard bully provoking a playground tussle. Beany fell into a soft snowbank. He stood up, brushed off his uniform, and swung at Drayton.

Drayton laughed out loud. "Look here, boys, the piano player wants a fight!" A scuffle broke out among the four men; they all rolled around in the snow, unable to keep their footing, with only a few blows finding their mark.

Ready to end the set-to, Drayton threw a hard left to Beany's face; his head snapped backwards and he fell to the ground unconscious.

"That'll give the little prick something to think on when he wakes up," Drayton said, rubbing his fist. "Load him in the back seat of his car — and Ralph, you drive." He picked up Beany's hat and tossed it in after him.

"But I thought it wouldn't start —"

"I'll give it a shove, it won't take much. You be ready to pop the clutch."

"Then what?" Ralph asked.

"Meet me at Chief's Gulley." Drayton drove around Beany's car and inched toward the back bumper. Slowly he began to push, careful not to damage his Moon. After only a few feet, the engine took hold. Drayton led the way out of town — winding around the ghostly countryside to Chief's Gulley. He parked just inside the open gate; Ralph pulled in behind. Both cars were left to idle.

"Give me a hand and we'll carry him down into the gulley proper," Drayton said, as they pulled Beany from his car.

"My feet's near froze," George said. "I'm for heading back to town."

"Hell, you're more of a pansy than this pretty soldier boy." Drayton took Beany's shoulders and Ralph his feet.

"This looks like Slip Stringer's old silver Buick," George said, as they approached the junk car; only the front grille was visible through the snow. "I was always partial to that Buick when it was running — the first silver car I ever seen."

"Lay him by the front bumper," Drayton said.

Ralph lost his hold and Beany dropped to the ground hard — rolling onto his stomach.

"Are you leaving him out here?" Ralph asked.

"It looks that way, don't it?"

"But he'll die —"

"Ain't you heard? Heroes don't die. Anyway, he'll wake up before he freezes to death; I didn't hit him *that* hard. And the walk home will do him good. Well, what are you waiting for? Drive Lafe's car back to town and park it in front of his house. Can you two geniuses handle that?"

"Whatever you say," they said in unison.

Drayton washed his hands with snow and drove home.

Chapter XXVIII

By the fall of 1945, all the men who had left Old Kane to fight in the war had returned one way or another. An even-dozen small white flags decorated windows around town, half with a blue star in the center for a son who went to war, half with a gold star for a son lost to that war.

Among Greene County's returning veterans was Asbury Wollums. As he stepped off the Jacksonville Trailways bus in Carrollton, he glanced at his watch: six P.M. The employees at the newspaper would be gone for the day. He would have time to look the place over before going home to Min.

Asbury walked around the familiar square, his collar pulled up against the cold, dank evening. A large "Welcome Home Soldiers" sign was nailed to a light pole, alongside a notice of a farm sale. All the stores were closed for the day, the sidewalks empty — a stroke of luck. The last thing he wanted was to run into an old acquaintance and be pulled into a long conversation.

Seeing his reflection in the store windows, Asbury wished he had not chosen to wear his uniform. That part of his life was over — except for the nightmares.

In the recurring dream he was back at Normandy, not carrying a gun, but a pencil and paper. He was running around the beach interviewing soldiers for the press service, asking them what they thought of the war and if they would be glad to get back home to their loved ones and how it felt to kill. Finally one soldier with half of his face blown off stood up and shouted, "Leave us alone! Can't you see we're all dead?" At that point Asbury would wake up shaking. He hoped the nightmares would stop once he went back to editing.

Asbury unlocked the front door of the newspaper office (he had carried the key to Europe and back), and stepped inside the dark building. In the years he was away, nothing had changed: a picture of the young Faulkner decorated one wall, tacked there his first day as editor; wastecans running over with crumpled paper; everywhere the smell of spilled ink. He opened the squeaky door to his old office; the hinges could use some oil. Tomorrow he would tend to such chores.

At the sound of the door opening, the slim, blond woman at the desk glanced up from the typewriter. Asbury looked twice before recognizing his wife.

"Az! Why didn't you let me know you were coming?" She walked toward her husband and kissed him lightly on the cheek. "I'm glad you made it home safe and sound." She was wearing the scent of wildflowers.

"A lot of guys didn't," he said, lamely. "Sorry I didn't write more, but things were pretty hectic." He had not expected to feel so ill at ease talking to his wife.

"I know. I read the newspapers." She smiled.

Asbury set his duffel bag on the desk and knocked over a vase of dried zinnias, scattering them onto her paperwork. He hastily cleaned up the mess. "Sorry to be so clumsy," he apologized. "How's the newspaper business these days?"

"Better than ever. I even got an award for one of my editorials. I meant to send you a copy."

He didn't bother to ask what the editorial had been about.

There was an awkward silence.

"You'll be glad to know I'm ready to take the helm again," Asbury said finally. "You can go back to being a housewife —"

"Az, I can't go back to being a housewife. The truth is, I can't go back to you."

Chapter XXIX

Nearly two years had passed since Beany Ozbun's death. By 1945, Cappy was the only person in Greene County still concerned with proving Drayton Hunt guilty of murder.

One evening on his way home from work, Cappy saw that Main Street was deserted — except for the royal-blue car parked in front of the barbershop. The vintage automobile glowed like a moonstone in the setting sun's light.

Cappy glanced inside the shop. Drayton Hunt, the last customer, was slouched in the large swivel chair puffing on a cigar as the barber put the finishing touches to his haircut.

On impulse, Cappy walked over to the Moon and looked inside. A large sack of groceries sat in the front passenger's seat, a sack of potatoes on the floor; Drayton's plaid jacket was draped across the top of the driver's seat. As Cappy was about to turn away, a small object dangling from the rearview mirror caught his eye. He pressed his nose against the window for a closer look; his heart began to pound.

Cappy ran into Pick's and telephoned Sheriff Perdun. The sheriff said he would take over from there. Cappy drove home as fast as the old Chevy would run to tell Worthy the news.

As he drove over the dusty road home, he thought about Beany. He wished his old friend was somewhere watching, to see Drayton Hunt pay for his crimes, but that wasn't likely.

As soon as he had hung up the phone with Cappy, Sheriff Perdun and his deputy, Specs Kirbach, drove directly to Mae Hunt's. Drayton's Moon was parked in front of the house. There it was, just as Cappy had said. A pink celluloid Kewpie doll hanging by a piece of twine, its head and body dented in from months of jostling over country roads. Two faint sets of initials were etched into the bottoms of the feet. "You're a witness to me finding this, Specs," he said to his deputy. "I'm surprised nobody noticed it till now." He cut the string, and stuffed the tiny doll into his uniform pocket. "We need to see a man about a doll."

Sheriff Perdun knocked on the front door of Mae's house.

Drayton came to the door wiping his hands on a dishtowel. "Well if it ain't Jesse Perdun and his shadow. What can I do for you?"

"Get your belongings, Drayton. You're coming with me."
"Now why would I be wanting to do that?"
"Because I'm putting you under arrest."
"What the hell for?"

"For the murder of Willa Giberson."

Drayton laughed out loud at the absurdity. "Jesus Christ, Jesse, you ain't serious —"

"Oh, I'm dead serious, you can bank on it and draw interest." He reached into his pocket and pulled out the doll. "This was hanging in your car. Can you explain how it came to be there?"

"I found it in the back seat of my Moon and thought it would look good hanging on the mirror. Where's the crime in that?"

"What would you say if I told you this doll once belonged to Willa Giberson?"

Drayton's face immediately sobered. "I'd say somebody's trying to frame me. I've did some acts I ain't too proud of over the years, Jesse, but I sure as hell didn't steal from no old lady or smother her, either!"

"That's for a judge and jury to think on. Get your things."

"I'll go," Drayton said, "but you'll be laughed out of town over this."

Drayton's mother stood on the back porch watching the sheriff take away her son. When she could no longer see the taillights of the sheriff's car, Mae fetched her "flower garden" quilt from her bed and carefully covered the Moon against the October chill — the closest she would come to returning Drayton's adoration.

WHEN WORTHY HEARD OF DRAYTON'S ARREST, he cranked his tractor to life and drove to Bum's, the throttle open full, a cloud of dust trying to keep up.

"I was about to head your way," Bum said, opening the door to his old friend. "You saved me a trip." Bum did not appear to be his usual cheerful self.

"It appears we've got some serious discussing to do. I reckon you heard the news about Hunt?"

"Who ain't? Take off your coat and set whilst I heat up the coffee." Bum stirred the fire and set the pot on top the hot stove.

"I'm facing a quandary, Bum. You and me both know Drayton Hunt didn't smother Willa. As much as I'd give to see that bastard locked up in jail, I feel bound to speak up at the trial."

"Have you talked this over with Cappy?"

"Nobody but you knows the truth of that night."

HIS FIRST NIGHT IN JAIL, Drayton lay awake considering his predicament. He knew he was innocent of the charge of murdering Willa Giberson, but trials sometimes go awry. By daylight he had a plan.

"I need to talk with Cappy Giberson," Drayton said when the sheriff brought his breakfast. He pulled a crumpled scrap of paper from his pocket and handed it to the sheriff. "What's on here is for Cappy's eyes only."

While the sheriff was away, Drayton considered what he would say to Cappy — a conversation he had anticipated for twenty years. He could never look at Cappy without thinking back to that day in Worthy's barn. Drayton could still smell the fresh-cut bales of hay and warm piles of fresh cow manure, mingled with the fresh girl-scent of Chastity Giberson.

CHASTITY HAD GONE TO THE BARN early that morning, hoping to get her chores finished before the day's heat set in. She scooped her apron full of corn and emptied it into buckets for the horses and mule, rubbing their necks affectionately as they began to eat. She pumped fresh water from the well into the trough. For the next half hour, she was busy with the animals, humming as she worked.

She was nearly finished when the barn door squeaked open, then closed. She turned to see Drayton Hunt ambling toward her.

"Hello, Missy," he said. "Fancy finding you all by your lonesome."

"Does Pa know you're here?"

"I ain't here to see your pa." He moved closer to her. "When I got up this morning, I thinks to myself, Today is a good day for a ride. Me and my Moon will mosey out to Worthy Giberson's place and see if that little girlie of his wants another trip through the countryside. Something tells me she liked it, even though she run off like a scared rabbit. So here we are, me and my Moon. Now how about that ride?"

"I had enough riding the other day." She started for the door.

"I'm willing to stay right here in the barn if that's what you want. We can have our little ride right here in the hay. What do you say to that?"

"I say you'd better be leaving before Pa catches you. I have to gather up eggs before the old hens break them." She put her hand on the barn-door latch, but Drayton stepped in front of her.

"Come on now, let's you and me have a little fun," he said, winking. "I've got a nice, big present for you." He grabbed her hand and placed it on his erection. "Go up in the loft with me and this is all yours."

Chastity allowed herself to be led up the ladder, and before she knew what was happening, he had mounted her like a boar on a shoat. Three loud grunts and he was finished. So that's what it's all about, Chastity thought with disappointment. She brushed the hay from her hair and clothes, wiped herself with the hem of her dress, and went to gather eggs.

Drayton had walked away from the barn chalking up another conquest. When he happened to see Chastity walking down the street pregnant a few months later, he realized she must not have told her folks or Worthy would have been after him with a shotgun.

THE SOUND OF FOOTSTEPS brought Drayton back to the present. Cappy unlocked the cell door and stepped inside.

"I reckon you and me has got some private matters to talk about," Drayton said.

"What did you mean by that note? 'If you want to meet your real pa, come to the jail.'"

"I thought it would explain itself." A grin spread across his clean-shaven face. He still smelled of *Old Spice*.

"I'm not in the mood for a guessing game. So where is he?" Cappy stared at the man standing in front of him. Seconds passed. Suddenly the meaning of the note became clear. But was it possible? Was this why Worthy hated Drayton Hunt so?

"I can see you're catching on. Now the question is, what are you going to do about it?"

"Why should I believe you? Where's the proof?" After years of wondering about his father, had it come to this?

"You've got your ma's face and hair color, but you and me's an exact match if you look at our frames. That's proof enough for any judge, crooked or fair."

Regretfully, Cappy could not argue either point. Suddenly he felt a new rage against this man. He grabbed him by the collar. "You bastard, if what you say is true, you're worse than I thought. My ma was nothing but a little girl!"

"I'll agree to being called a bastard, but that's another way we're alike, you and me — both bastards."

Cappy let go of his collar and took a shaky step back.

"Except now you know who your pa is," Drayton said, straightening his collar, "and I'll likely never know mine. But this late in the game it don't matter. As for forcing your ma, there wasn't no forcing to it. All I done was show up at the barn one day and found her ripe as a summer peach."

Cappy ached at the thought. "Why are you coming out with this now?"

"I always meant to tell you. Worthy's knowed about me from the day of your ma's funeral, but he's too damned stubborn to believe me. Since I done you the favor of bringing you into this world, I'm ready to collect on that favor by asking one back."

"Keep going."

"My pecker's in a vise over that damned Kewpie doll. It wouldn't take more than a little white lie to help me out; it don't have to be bald-faced. Hell, you know what to do, just write something for the paper and throw in some words to muddy the waters and raise a doubt or two. Do that and my lips is sealed about that day in the barn. What do you say?"

For once, Cappy was at a loss for words. As a child, he had taken liberties with the truth to gain the respect of his peers, and the newspaper writing called for embellishing the truth now and then in the interest of a better story — but this was another matter.

"I can't give you an answer now," Cappy said. "I'll drop by the jail in a day or so."

When worthy got in from the fields, Cappy was waiting on the porch step, his head down. "What is it, Cap? You look like you lost your job."

Cappy looked up. "Sometimes finding something is as bad as losing something."

"Back up there, boy, and talk plain Old Kane English."

"Drayton Hunt claims he's my real pa. What's more, he says you know all about it and always have. Is he telling the truth?" Cappy looked steadily at Worthy.

The question Worthy had been dreading for nearly two decades was upon him, but he still had no easy answer. "I'll be real honest with you, Cap, I don't know. In spite of Hunt's claims, I figured your pa was a stranger passing through the countryside and just let it go at that. Some would say we stuck our heads in the sand. Then when you was born and your real ma passed, taking the secret with her, there didn't seem to be no use in worrying the issue. But why did that weasel pick now for making the claim?"

"Bribery. He says if I agree to write an item for the paper and plant the idea that *maybe* he's being framed, he won't tell the town that he's my pa. I don't want to claim him as kin and let him slander my real mother, but I can't let him get away with smothering the ma who raised me!"

The older man sighed and dropped onto the porch step. He put an arm around the boy's shoulder. "Cap, it breaks my heart, but there's something else that needs telling, and after you hear what I've got to say you may disown me and claim Hunt."

Worthy disclosed the events of the night of the 1944 March of Dimes Dance. He pulled a bandanna from his pocket and wiped his eyes, that snowy January night still weighing heavily on him.

Cappy sat quietly at Worthy's feet, wishing he were still a six-year-old boy removing the light from a lightning bug. He had grown up listening to tall tales, the fun being that he never knew for sure whether a story was whimsy or gospel, but Cappy knew this was no tall tale. "Don't wait supper," he said suddenly, his decision made. "And Pa, you did the right thing."

DRAYTON WAS SITTING ON THE COT when Cappy opened the cell door. "I knew you'd show up," Drayton said, grinning self-assuredly. "Hell, when it comes down to it, you're no different than me. Like father, like son."

"This won't take long. I sure as shit don't want you telling we're kin, but I know you killed Beany Ozbun, the best friend I'll ever have, and I can't let that pass. Now if seeing justice done means engaging in a bit of storytelling on my part, so be it. In case you haven't figured it out, the moral of my story will be that a man always pays for the bad he does."

Drayton jumped up from the cot, and yelled in Cappy's face. "You'll set by and let me go to jail for smothering Willa Giberson? You know I never done that deed!"

"Whether you put a pillow over Ma's face doesn't matter one whit. What matters is we both know that one way or another you're guilty of murdering Beany. You of all people should see the humor here. This ends our business. I expect I'll be seeing you in court. And one more thing. My real pa was a farm worker passing through the countryside. That's what Pa said and that's what I believe."

"You and Worthy ain't fooling nobody but yourselves," Drayton sneered.

Chapter XXX

$\widehat{}$

$\mathcal{A}$t the trial of Drayton R. Hunt, every seat in the courtroom was taken, with the overflow of spectators standing around the walls. The men of the jury were eager to convict the defendant so they could return to their farms and stores.

The prosecution set out to prove that on the night of January 20, 1944 following the March of Dimes Dance, Drayton Hunt had stopped at Oettle's Tavern for a beer, and then had driven to the Worthy Giberson home. The prosecution's entire case was based on the Kewpie doll, which Drayton had allegedly picked up as a souvenir after finishing off Willa. Except for the beer at Oettle's, the rest was speculation.

Worthy was called to identify the doll. He pointed out the initials "WG and WC," scratched on the bottom of the tiny pink feet, which stood for Worthy Giberson and Willa Cope. The doll was then passed to the jury so they could examine it for themselves.

Buck Oettle verified that Drayton had been in his establishment after the March of Dimes Dance drinking beer, but he could not say with any certainty whether he went directly home afterward.

The defense claimed that on the night in question, Drayton Hunt left the dance, had a beer at Oettle's Tavern, and went home to be with his mother, who was ill. Mae Hunt substantiated her son's alibi. What was a mother to do?

Other than Mae, Burley Walk was the only witness for the defense. Burley swore on the Bible that he had seen the doll in George Woosley's pocket, even pinpointing the place and exact time of day. But when he was excused from the witness chair, he pledged allegiance to the flag and giggled all the way back to his seat. The jury would view his testimony with skepticism, and would conclude that Drayton had given Burley a nickel to implicate George.

As for the doll, Drayton swore he found it in the back seat of his Moon, and had hung it on his mirror for a decoration. Drayton was between a rock and a hard place, and he knew it. He and the twins had already sworn that they were not together in the Moon the night of the dance. If he changed the story to accommodate the possibility that George had left the doll in his car, or put it there on purpose, the twins might be tricked into telling what they knew about Chief's Gulley. And being accused of *that* crime could turn out worse for him. He convinced his lawyer not to call Ralph and George in his defense.

Finding Drayton Hunt guilty of Willa Giberson's murder took the six men thirty-one minutes.

IN SPITE OF HIS LAWYER'S REPEATED WARNINGS, Drayton had sat during the trial chuckling at the irony of his predicament. And when the foreman read the verdict, he laughed out loud.

Judge Jurnikan asked the defendant to stand for pronouncement of the sentence: "Drayton R. Hunt, you have been found guilty of the murder of Willa Giberson. Is there anything you want to say in your own defense that didn't come out in this trial?"

"I sure as hell do have something to say." He had stopped laughing. "I swear I never smothered Willa Giberson. There's a party in this very room who knows that's gospel, but he's too much of a pansy to set the story straight. So I'll take my unjust punishment like a man."

"Drayton Hunt, I've known you since you were a boy," the judge said. "I know you didn't have it easy growing up, but a lot of us didn't. Since the evidence against you is circumstantial, the law will be lenient. You are hereby sentenced to three years in the Marion Penitentiary."

FOR CAPPY, IT WAS A BITTERSWEET VICTORY. But justice has its own way. As Worthy liked to say, "Life has a good many twists and turns, and if a man ain't watchful, he's likely to run smack dab into past deeds careening back at him."

Cappy worked the rest of the night at the newspaper office writing an account of the trial that would win him the "Young Journalist's Award of 1945".

DRAYTON DIDN'T SLEEP WELL his first night in Marion Penitentiary. The mattress was lumpy and sometime during the night a late fall thunderstorm commenced. As his eyes adjusted to the meager light of a solitary bulb in the hallway, he looked around his new home. The only civilities were a lavatory and toilet, and a small table that held a Gideon Bible.

The thunder grew louder, the lightning close; rain pelted the metal roof like buck shot. He walked to the barred window and stood on tiptoes to look out. He thought about his elegant old Moon left to sit through the frigid winters and blistering summers. Even though it was under a lean-to covered with his ma's quilt, time would take its toll. Drayton knew he would survive the years ahead, but when he walked out the front gate a free man, his Moon would be ready for Chief's Gulley.

He turned from the window like a man turning from the coffin of a loved one. The judge had rendered him impotent, made his castration clean and complete. The one thing that was his, that he loved, had been taken from him. He began to pace the tiny cell, shouting obscenities. "That son-of-a bitching judge! That cocksucker! He knows I never killed that old woman. He had it in for me, him and that fat sheriff, even that holier-than-thou boy of mine. They'll live to regret what they done, all of them." In despair, he sat on the cot, his head in his hands. For the first time since he was a baby, Drayton wept.

THE NOVEMBER MORNING PROMISED A FROSTY DAY, the sun beginning its shortened trip across the clear Illinois sky. The regulars were gathered around Pick's woodstove. Moods ran high.

"Drink up, fellas." Pick smiled as he filled each man's cup to the brim. "Coffee's back in force!"

Bum swished the coffee around in his mouth, then swallowed. "Now that's what I call coffee! While the war was on, we was getting the dregs of the barrel."

"The paper says they're starting to build new cars again," Pick said.

"And *Gangbusters* is coming back to the air waves," Worthy said, recalling the claim that it encouraged crime. "I guess the bigwigs think we've growed up during the war."

"I'd say in general most things are on their way back to where they once stood," Pick said.

"Not for Drayton Hunt, they ain't," Bum said. The others nodded in agreement. "He's been cooling his heels in Marion for a month."

"The way he took on at the trial was the damnedest thing I ever viewed," Pick said. "That crazy laughing didn't go to help his cause one iota."

"I'll wager he ain't laughing now," Bum said. "Say, Worthy, what ever happened to that Kewpie doll?"

"She's back setting on the hallway table good as new, save a dent here and there."

"There's something bothering me about that doll," Pick said. "If it was hanging in Hunt's car for close to two years, you'd think during all that time somebody would have seen it dangling there in plain sight."

"Well," said Worthy, "that doll ain't much bigger than my

thumb. It's not easy to spot. Lucky for us, nothing much gets past Cappy once he sets his sights."

"That Cappy's a natural-born newshawk, all right," Pick said. "You raised a mighty fine boy, Worthy."

"I can't take all the credit," Worthy answered, feeling a father's pride. "Willa done her part as long as she was able." He drained his cup and set it on the counter, then stood up and lazily stretched his arms. "Well, Bum, let's you and me head for the creek bank before the freeze gets all the bluegill. This good weather won't last forever." He walked out the door with Bum limping along behind.

"I've got a question for you," Cappy said as he and Worthy were doing breakfast dishes the next morning.

"I can't guarantee I'll know the answer, but I'll give her my best try."

"It's about going off to school. Before Asbury hired me at the paper, he made me promise I'd get some college when the war was over, and lately Min's started singing the same tune. Now that the time's come I'm not much for it. There's never a day that somebody doesn't tell me how much they like my writing. I think I'm good enough without four years of college. What do you think?"

Worthy was caught off-guard, and he nearly dropped Willa's favorite mashed-potato bowl. This marked only the second time Cappy had asked his advice, the first being when he wanted to work for the newspaper after winning the eighth-grade essay contest. And he hadn't heeded his advice then.

"There's all kinds of education, Cap," Worthy began. "I didn't get much education from a schoolroom; mine mostly come from everyday dealings. Anymore, people confuse schooling with being smart."

Cappy knew he was in for a lengthy explanation.

"I had a friend once, you never knowed him as he was before your time, but we was boyhood pals, something like you and Beany. Roscoe Jones was his name. Roscoe was a piano player of no equal. He could set down at a piano, didn't matter if it was a grand piano or upright, and he could make them keys fairly talk. He could set for hours and never play the same song twice. Couldn't read a note of music, didn't need to. Roscoe was proud of that fact."

"My question was about writing, not piano playing."

"Give me time and I'll get there. Well, Roscoe's ma took it into her head that he needed 'proper training'; them was her very words. So she scrimped and saved and Roscoe went off to college. Well, by the time he graduated, he couldn't brag no more about not playing music by note. No, by God, Roscoe Jones had spent four years playing nothing *but* notes, them professors being real sticklers about that.

"You see, note-playing stiffened Roscow to where he wasn't fit to play a real tune. And somewhere in those four years he lost his rhythm to boot. You couldn't tap your foot to what he played for love nor money. The way I see it, if everybody played the piano by notes, they'd all sound alike and nobody would stand out special.

"Now it occurs to me that college can do the same for a man who wants to write stories. Take you. Words come out of you without you giving them much thought. My greatest fear is that four years of higher schooling would stiffen them words to where a plain man won't know what you're getting at —"

"Thanks for your advice, Pa." Cappy turned to leave, not waiting for Worthy to finish.

"Where you off to?"

"To see about signing up for college. If I hurry, maybe I can get in second semester." He was out the door.

"Damn, but I'm good," Worthy chuckled. He put the last dish away, and hung up the dishtowel to dry.